George Manville Fenn

The Master of the Ceremonies

Vol. I

George Manville Fenn

The Master of the Ceremonies
Vol. I

ISBN/EAN: 9783337066154

Printed in Europe, USA, Canada, Australia, Japan

Cover: Foto ©Andreas Hilbeck / pixelio.de

More available books at **www.hansebooks.com**

THE MASTER OF THE CEREMONIES.

THE

MASTER OF THE CEREMONIES.

A Novel.

BY

GEORGE MANVILLE FENN,

AUTHOR OF 'DOUBLE CUNNING,' 'THE PARSON O' DUMFORD,' ETC., ETC.

IN THREE VOLUMES.

VOL. I.

London:

WARD AND DOWNEY,

YORK STREET, COVENT GARDEN.

1886.

CONTENTS OF VOL. I.

———◆◆———

THE
MASTER OF THE CEREMONIES.

CHAPTER I.

HIS HOUSE.

EARLY morning at Saltinville, with the tide down, and the calm sea shimmering like damasked and deadened silver in the sunshine. Here and there a lugger was ashore, delivering its take of iris-hued mackerel to cart and basket, as a busy throng stood round, some upon the sands, some knee-deep in water, and all eager to obtain a portion of the fresh fish that fetched so good a price amongst the visitors to the town.

The trawler was coming in, too, with its freight of fine thick soles and turbot, with a few gaily-scaled red mullet; and perhaps a staring-eyed John Dory or two, from the trammel net set overnight amongst the rocks: all choice fish, these, to be bought up ready for royal and noble use, for London would see no scale of any of the fish caught that night.

The unclouded sun flashed from the windows of the houses on the cliff, giving them vivid colours that the decorator had spared, and lighting up the downs beyond, so that from the sea Saltinville looked a very picture of all that was peaceful and bright. There were no huge stucco palaces to mar the landscape, for all was modest as to architecture, and as fresh as green and stone-coloured paint applied to window-frame, veranda and shutter could make it. Flowers of variety were not plentiful, but great clusters of orange marigolds flourished bravely, and, with broad-disked sunflowers, did no little towards giving warmth of colour to the place. There had been no storms of late—no windy nights when the spray was torn from the tops of waves to fly in showers over the houses, and beat the window-panes, crusting them afterwards with a coat of dingy salt. The windows, then, were flashing in the sun ; but all the same, by six o'clock, Isaac Monkley, the valet, body-servant, and footman-in-ordinary to Stuart Denville, Esquire, M.C., was busy, dressed in a striped jacket, and standing on the very top of a pair of steps, cloth in one hand and wash-leather in the other, carefully cleaning windows that were already spotless. For there was something in the exterior of the M.C.'s house that suggested its tenant. Paint, glass, walls, and doorstep were so scrupulously clean that they recalled the master's face, and seemed to have been clean-shaven but an hour before.

Isaac was not alone in his task, for, neat in a print dress and snowy cap, Eliza, the housemaid, was standing on a chair within; and as they cleaned the windows in concert, they courted in a special way.

There is no accounting for the pleasure people find in very ordinary ways. Isaac and Eliza found theirs in making the glass so clear that they could smile softly at each other without let or hindrance produced by smear or speck in any single pane. Their hands, too, were kept in contact, saving for cloth and glass, and moved in unison, describing circles and a variety of other figures, going into the corners together, changing from cloth to wash-leather, and moving, as it were, by one set of muscles till the task was concluded with a chaste salute—a kiss through the glass.

Meanwhile, anyone curious about the house would, if he had raised his eyes, have seen that one of the upstairs windows had a perfect screen of flowers, that grew from a broad, green box along the sill. Sweet peas clustered, roses bloomed, geraniums dotted it with brilliant tiny pointless stars of scarlet, and at one side there was a string that ran up from a peg to a nail, hammered, unknown to the M.C., into the wall. That peg was an old tooth-brush handle, and the nail had been driven in with the back of a hair-brush; but bone handle and string were invisible now,

1—2

covered by the twining strands of so many ipomæas, whose
heart-shaped leaves and trumpet blossoms formed one of
the most lovely objects of the scene.   Here they were of
richest purple, fading into lavender and grey ; there of delicate pink with well-formed starry markings in the inner
bell, and moist with the soft air of early morning.   Each
blossom was a thing of beauty soon to fade, for, as the
warm beams of the sun kissed them, the edges began to
curl ; then there would be a fit of shrivelling, and the bloom
of the virgin flower passed under the sun-god's too ardent
caress.

About and above this screen of flowers, a something ivory
white, and tinged with peachy pink, kept darting in and out.
Now it touched a rose, and a shower of petals fell softly
down ; now a geranium leaf that was turning yellow disappeared ; now again a twig that had borne roses was taken
away, after a sound that resembled a steely click.   Then
the little crimson and purple blossoms of a fuchsia were
touched, and shivered and twinkled in the light at the soft
movements among the graceful stems as dying flowers were
swept away.

For a minute again all was still, but the next, there was a
fresh vibration amongst the flowers as this ivory whiteness
appeared in a new place, curving round a plant as if in
loving embrace ; and at such times the blooms seemed drawn
towards another and larger flower of thicker petal and of

coral hue, that peeped out amongst the fresh green leaves, and then it was that a watcher would have seen that this ivory something playing about the window garden was a soft white hand.

Again a fresh vibration amongst the clustering flowers, as if they were trembling with delight at the touches that were once more to come. Then there was a brilliant flash as the sun's rays glanced from a bright vessel, the pleasant gurgle of water from a glass carafe, and once more stillness before the stems were slowly parted, and a larger flower peeped out from the leafy screen—the soft, sweet face of Claire Denville—to gaze at the sea and sky, and inhale the morning air.

Richard Linnell was not there to look up and watch the changes in the sweet, candid face, with its high white forehead, veined with blue, its soft, peachy cheeks and clear, dark-grey eyes, full of candour, but searching and firm beneath the well-marked brows. Was her mouth too large? Perhaps so ; but what a curve to that upper lip, what a bend to the lower over that retreating dimpled chin. If it had been smaller the beauty of the regular teeth would have been more hidden, and there would have been less of the pleasant smile that came as Claire brushed aside her wavy brown hair, turned simply back, and knotted low down upon her neck.

Pages might be written in Claire Denville's praise : let it

suffice that she was a tall, graceful woman, and that even the most disparaging scandalmonger of the place owned that she was 'not amiss.'

Claire Denville's gaze out to sea was but a short one. Then her face disappeared; the stems and blossoms darted back to form a screen, and the tenant of the barely-furnished bedroom was busy for some time, making the bed and placing all in order before drawing a tambour frame to the window, and unpinning a piece of paper that guarded the gay silks and wools. Then for the next hour Claire bent over her work, the glistening needle passing rapidly in and out as she gazed intently at the pattern rapidly approaching completion, a piece of work that was to be taken surreptitiously to Miss Clode's library and fancy bazaar for sale, money being a scarce commodity in the M.C.'s home.

From below, time after time, came up sounds of preparation for the breakfast of the domestics, then for their own, and Claire sighed as she thought of the expenses incurred for three servants, and how much happier they might be if they lived in simpler style.

The chiming of the old church clock sounded sweetly on the morning air.

Ting-dong—quarter-past; and Claire listened attentively.

Ting-dong—half-past.

Ting-dong—quarter to eight.

'How time goes!' she cried, with a wistful look at her

work, which she hurriedly covered, and then her print dress rustled as she ran downstairs to find her father already in the little pinched parlour, dubbed breakfast-room, standing thin and pensive in a long faded dressing-gown, one arm resting upon the chimney-piece, snuff-box in hand, the other raised level with his face, holding the freshly-dipped-for pinch—in fact, standing in a studied attitude, as if for his portrait to be limned.

CHAPTER II.

'Ah, my child, you are late,' said the Master of the Ceremonies, as Claire ran to meet him and kissed his cheek.
'"Early to bed and early to rise makes a man healthy,
wealthy, and wise." It will do the same for you, my child,
and add bloom to your cheek, though, of course, we cannot
be early in the season.'

'I am a little late, papa dear,' said Claire, ringing a
tinkling bell, with the result that Isaac, in his striped jacket
and the stiffest of white cravats, entered, closed the door
behind him, and then stood statuesque, holding a brightly-
polished kettle, emitting plenty of steam.

'Any letters, Isaac?'

'No, sir, none this morning,' and then Isaac carefully
poured a small quantity of the boiling water into the teapot,
whose lid Claire had raised, and stood motionless while she
poured it out again, and then unlocked a very small tea-
caddy and spooned out three very small spoonfuls—one

apiece, and none for the over-cleaned and de-silvered plated pot. This done, Isaac filled up, placed the kettle on the hob, fetched a Bible and prayer-book from a sideboard, placed them at one end of the table and went out.

' Why is not Morton down ?' said the M.C. sternly.

' He came down quite an hour ago, papa. He must have gone for a walk. Shall we wait ?'

' Certainly not, my child.'

At that moment there was a little scuffling outside the door, which was opened directly after by Isaac, who admitted Eliza and a very angular-looking woman with two pins tightly held between her lips—pins that she had intended to transfer to some portion of her garments, but had not had time. These three placed themselves before three chairs by the door, and waited till the M.C. had gracefully replaced his snuff-box, and taken two steps to the table, where he and Claire sat down. Then the servants took their seats, and then ' Master ' opened the Bible to read in a slow, deliberate way, and as if he enjoyed the names, that New Testament chapter on genealogies which to youthful ears seemed to be made up of a constant repetition of the two words, ' which was.'

This ended, all rose and knelt down, Isaac with the point of his elbow just touching the point of Eliza's elbow, for he comforted his conscience over this tender advance by the reflection that marriage, though distant, was a sacred thing; and he made up for his unspiritual behaviour to a great extent by saying the ' Amens ' in a much louder voice than Cook, and finished off in the short space of silence after the Master of the Ceremonies had read the last Collect, and when all were expected to continue their genuflexions till that personage sighed and made a movement as if to rise, by adding a short extempore prayer of his own, one which he had repeated religiously for the past four years without effect, the supplication being:

' And finally, may we all get the arrears of our wages, evermore.   Amen.'

Isaac had finished his supplementary prayer; the M.C. sighed and rose, and, the door being opened by the footman, the two maids stepped out.   Isaac followed, and in a few minutes returned with a very coppery rack, containing four thin pieces of toast, and a little dish whose contents were hidden by a very battered cover.   These were placed with the greatest form upon the table, and the cover removed with a flourish, to reveal two very thin and very curly pieces of streaky bacon, each of which had evidently been trying to inflate itself like the frog in the fable, but with no other result than the production of a fatty bladdery puff, supported by a couple of patches of brown.

Isaac handed the toast to father and daughter, and then went off with the cover silently as a spirit, and the breakfast was commenced by the M.C. softly breaking a piece of toast with his delicate fingers and saying :

' I am displeased with Morton. After yesterday's incident, he should have been here to discuss with me the future of his campaign.'

' Here he is, papa,' cried Claire eagerly, and she rose to kiss her brother affectionately as he came rather boisterously into the room, looking tall, thin and pale, but healthy and hungry, as an overgrown boy of nineteen would look who had been out at the seaside before breakfast.

' You were not here to prayers, Morton,' said the M.C. sternly.

' No, father ; didn't know it was so late,' said the lad, beginning on the toast as soon as he was seated.

' I trust that you have not been catching—er—er—dabs, this morning.' The word was distasteful when the fish was uncooked, and required an effort to enunciate.

' Oh, but I have, though. Rare sport this morning. Got enough for dinner.'

The M.C. was silent for a few moments, and gracefully sipped his thin tea. He was displeased, but there was a redeeming feature in his son's announcement—enough fish for dinner. There would be no need to order anything of the butcher.

' Hush, Morton,' said Claire softly, and she laid her soft little hand on his, seeing their father about to speak.

' I am—er—sorry that you should be so thoughtless,

Morton,' said his father; 'at a time, too, when I am making unheard-of efforts to obtain that cornetcy for you; how can you degrade yourself—you, the son of a—er—man—a—er —gentleman in my position, by going like a common boy down below that pier to catch—er—dabs!'

'Well, we want them,' retorted the lad. 'A good dinner of dabs isn't to be sneezed at. I'm as hungry as hungry, sometimes. See how thin I am. Why, the boys laugh, and call me Lanky Denville.'

'What is the opinion of boys to a young man with your prospects in life?' said his father, carefully ignoring the question of food supply. 'Besides, you ought to be particular, sir, for the sake of your sister May, who has married so well.'

'What, to jerry-sneaky Frank Burnett? A little humbug.'

'Morton!'

'Well, so he is, father. I asked him to lend me five shillings the day before yesterday, and he called me an importunate beggar.'

'You had no business to ask him for money, sir.'

'Who am I to ask, then? I must have money. You won't let me go out to work.'

'No, sir; you are a gentleman's son, and must act as a gentleman.'

'I can't act as a gentleman without money,' cried the lad, eating away, for, to hide the look of pain in her face, Claire kept diligently attending to her brother's wants by supplying him with a fair amount of thin tea and bread and butter, as well as her own share of the bacon.

'My dear son,' said the M.C. with dignity, 'everything comes to the man who will wait. Your sister May has made a wealthy marriage. Claire will, I have no doubt, do the same, and I have great hopes of your prospects.'

'Haven't any prospects,' said the lad, in an ill-used tone.

'Not from me,' said the M.C., 'for I am compelled to keep up appearances before the world, and my fees and offerings are not nearly so much as people imagine.'

'Then why don't we live accordingly?' said the lad roughly.

'Allow me, with my experience, sir, to know best; and I desire that you will not take that tone towards me. Recollect, sir, that I am your father.'

'Indeed, dear papa, Morton does not mean to be disrespectful.'

'Silence, Claire. And you, Morton; I will be obeyed.'

'All right, father. I'll obey fast enough, but it does seem precious hard to see Ikey down in the kitchen stuffing himself, and us up in the parlour going short so as to keep up appearances.'

'My boy,' said the M.C. pathetically, 'it is Spartan-like. It is self-denying and manly. Have courage, and all will end well. I know it is hard. It is my misfortune, but I appeal to you both, do I ever indulge myself at your expense? Do I ever spare myself in my efforts for you?'

'No, no, no, dear,' cried Claire, rising with tears in her eyes to throw her arm round his neck and kiss him.

'Good girl!—good girl!' he said, smiling sadly, and returning the embrace. 'But sit down, sit down now, and let us discuss these very weighty matters. Fortune is beginning to smile upon us, my dears. May is off my hands—well married.'

Claire shook her head sadly.

'I say well married, Claire,' said her father sternly, 'and though we have still that trouble ever facing us, of a member of our family debauched by drunkenness, and sunk down to the degradation of a common soldier——'

'Oh! I say, father, leave poor old Fred alone,' cried Morton. 'He isn't a bad fellow; only unlucky.'

'Be silent, sir, and do not mention his name again in my presence. And Claire, once for all, I forbid his coming to this house.'

'He only came to the back door,' grumbled Morton.

'A son who is so degraded that he cannot come to the front door, and must lower himself to the position of one of our servants, is no companion for my children. I forbid all further communication with him.'

'Oh, papa!' cried Claire, with the tears in her eyes.

'Silence! Morton, my son, I have hopes that by means

of my interest a certain person will give you a commission
in the Light Dragoons, and—For what we have received
may the Lord make us truly thankful.'

'Amen,' said Morton. 'Claire, I want some more bread
and butter.'

'Claire,' said the Master of the Ceremonies, rising from
the table as a faint tinkle was heard, 'there is the Countess's
bell.'

He drew the girl aside and laid a thin white finger upon
her shoulder.

'You must give her a broader hint this morning, Claire.
Six months, and she has paid nothing whatever. I cannot,
I really cannot go on finding her ladyship in apartments and
board like this. It is so unreasonable. A woman, too, with
her wealth. Pray, speak to her again, but don't offend her
You must be careful. Delicately, my child—delicately. A
leader of fashion even now. A woman of exquisite refinement. Of the highest aristocracy. Speak delicately. It
would never do to cause her annoyance about such a sordid
thing as money—a few unsettled debts of honour. Ah, her
bell again. Don't keep her waiting.'

'If you please, ma'am, her ladyship has rung twice,' said
Isaac, entering the room; 'and Eliza says shall she go?'

'No, Isaac, your mistress will visit her ladyship,' said the
M.C. with dignity. 'You can clear away, Isaac—you can
clear away.'

Stuart Denville, Esquire, walked to the window and took
a pinch of snuff. As soon as his back was turned Isaac
grinned and winked at Morton, making believe to capture
and carry off the bread and butter; while the lad hastily
wrote on a piece of paper :

'Pour me out a cup of tea in the pantry, Ike, and I'll
come down.'

Five minutes later the room was cleared, and the M.C.
turned from the window to catch angrily from the table some
half-dozen letters which the footman had placed ready for
him to see.

'Bills, bills, bills,' he said, in a low, angry voice, thrusting
them unread into the drawer of a cabinet; 'what am I to
do? How am I to pay?'

He sat down gracefully, as if it were part of his daily life,
and his brow wrinkled, and an old look came into his face
as he thought of the six months' arrears of the lady who
occupied his first floor, and his hands began to tremble
strangely as he seemed to see open before him an old-
fashioned casket, in which lay, glittering upon faded velvet,
necklet, tiara, brooch, earrings and bracelets — large
diamonds of price; a few of which, if sold, would be sufficient to pay his debts, and enable him to keep up appearances, and struggle on, till Claire was well married, and
his son well placed.

Money—money—always struggling on for money in this

life of beggarly gentility ; while only on the next floor that old woman on the very brink of the grave had trinkets, any one of which——

He made a hasty gesture, as if he were thrusting back some temptation, and took up a newspaper, but let it fall upon his knees as his eyes lit upon a list of bankrupts.

Was it come to that ? He was heavily in debt to many of the tradespeople. The epidemic in the place last year had kept so many people away, and his fees had been less than ever. Things still looked bad. Then there was the rent, and Barclay had said he would not wait, and there were the bills that Barclay held—his acceptances for money borrowed at a heavy rate to keep up appearances when his daughter May—his idol—the pretty little sunbeam of his house—became Mrs. Frank Burnett.

' Barclay is hard, very hard,' said the Master of the Ceremonies to himself. ' Barclay said——'

He again made that gesture, a gracefully made gesture of repelling something with his thin, white hands, but the thought came back.

' Barclay said that half the ladies of fashion when short of money, through play, took their diamonds to their jeweller, sold some of the best, and had them replaced with paste. It took a connoisseur to tell the difference by candle-light.'

Stuart Denville, poverty-stricken gentleman, the poorest

of men, suffering as he did the misery of one struggling to keep up appearances, rose to his feet with a red spot in each of his cheeks, and a curious look in his eyes.

'No, no,' he ejaculated excitedly as he walked up and down, ' a gentleman, sir—a gentleman, if poor. Better one's razors or a pistol. They would say it was all that I could do. Not the first gentleman who has gone to his grave like that.'

He shuddered and stood gazing out of the window at the sea, which glittered in the sunshine like—yes, like diamonds.

Barclay said he had often changed diamonds for paste, and no one but a judge could tell what had been done. Half a dozen of the stones from a bracelet replaced with paste, and he would be able to hold up his head for a year, and by that time how changed everything might be.

Curse the diamonds ! Was he mad ? Why did the sea dance and sparkle, and keep on flashing like brilliants ? Was it the work of some devil to tempt him with such thoughts ? Or was he going mad ?

He took pinch after pinch of snuff, and walked up and down with studied dancing-master strides as if he were being observed, instead of alone in that shabby room, and as he walked he could hear the dull buzz of voices and a light tread overhead.

He walked to the window again with a shudder, and the sea still seemed to be all diamonds.

He could not bear it, but turned to his seat, into which he sank heavily, and covered his face with his hands.

Diamonds again—glistening diamonds, half a dozen of which, taken—why not borrowed for a time from the old woman who owed him so much, and would not pay? Just borrowed for the time, and paste substituted till fate smiled upon him, and his plans were carried out. How easy it would be. And she, old, helpless, would never know the difference—and it was to benefit his children.

'I cannot bear it,' he moaned; and then, 'Barclay would do it for me. He is secret as the tomb. He never speaks. If he did, what reputations he could blast.'

So easy; the old woman took her opiate every night, and slept till morning. She would not miss the cross—yes, that would be the one—no, a bracelet better. She never wore that broad bracelet, Claire said, now she had realized that her arms were nothing but bone.

'Am I mad?' cried the old man, starting up again. 'Yes, what is it?'

'Messenger from Mr. Barclay, sir, to say he will call to-morrow at twelve, and he hopes you will be in.'

'Yes, yes, Isaac; say yes, I will be in,' said the wretched man, sinking back in his chair with the perspiration starting out all over his brow. And then, as he was left alone, 'How am I to meet him? What am I to say?' he whispered. 'Oh, it is too horrible to bear!'

Once more he started to his feet and walked to the window and looked out upon the sea.

Diamonds—glittering diamonds as far as eye could reach, and the Master of the Ceremonies, realizing more and more the meaning of the word temptation, staggered away from the window with a groan.

CHAPTER III.

THE FLICKERING FLAME.

'DRAW the curtains, my dear, and then go into the next room, and throw open the French window quite wide.'

It was a mumbling noise that seemed to come out of a cap-border lying on a pillow, for there was no face visible; but a long thin elevation of the bedclothes, showing that some one was lying there, could be seen in the dim light.

Claire drew the curtains, opened a pair of folding doors, and crossed the front room to open the French window and admit the sweet fresh air.

She stepped out into the balcony supported by wooden posts, up which a creeper was trained, and stood by a few shrubs in pots gazing out at the brilliant sea; but only for a few moments, before turning, recrossing the skimpily furnished drawing-room, and going into the back, where the large four-post bedstead suddenly began to quiver, and the bullion fringe all round to dance, as its occupant burst into a spasmodic fit of coughing.

'He—he—he, hi—hi—hi, hec—hec—hec, ha—ha—ha! ho—ho! Bless my—hey—ha! hey—ha! hugh—hugh— hugh! Oh dear me! oh—why don't you—heck—heck— heck—heck—heck! Shut the—ho—ho—ho—ho—hugh— hugh—window before I—ho—ho—ho—ho!'

Claire flew back across the drawing-room and shut the window, hurrying again to the bedside, where, as she drew aside the curtains, the morning light displayed a ghastly-looking, yellow-faced old woman, whose head nodded and bowed in a palsied manner, as she sat up, supporting herself with one arm, and wiped her eyes—the hand that held the handkerchief being claw-like and bony, and covered with a network of prominent veins.

She was a repulsive-looking, blear-eyed old creature, with a high-bridged aquiline nose that seemed to go with the claw-like hand. A few strands of white hair had escaped from beneath the great mob of lace that frilled her night-cap, and hung over forehead and cheek, which were lined and wrinkled like a walnut shell, only ten times as deeply.

'It's—it's your nasty damp house,' mumbled the old woman spitefully, her lips seeming to be drawn tightly over her gums, and her nose threatening to tap her chin as she spoke. 'It's—it's killing me. I never had such a cough before. D—n Saltinville! I hate it.'

'Oh, Lady Teigne, how can you talk like that!' cried Claire. 'It is so shocking.'

'What! to say d——? 'Tisn't. I'll say it again. A hundred times if I like;' and she rattled out the condemnatory word a score of times over, as fast as she could utter it, while Claire looked on in a troubled way at the hideous old wretch before her.

'Well, what are you staring at, pink face! Wax doll! Baby chit! Don't look at me in that proud way, as if you were rejoicing because you are young, and I am a little old. You'll be like me some day. If you live—he—he—he! If you live. But you won't. You look consumptive. Eh?'

'I did not speak,' said Claire sadly. 'Shall I bring your breakfast, Lady Teigne?'

'Yes, of course. Are you going to starve me? Mind the beef-tea's strong this morning, and put a little more cognac in, child. Don't you get starving me. Tell your father, child, that I shall give him a cheque some day. I haven't forgotten his account, but he is not to pester me with reminders. I shall pay him when I please.'

'My father would be greatly obliged, Lady Teigne, if you would let him have some money at once. I know he is pressed.'

'How dare you! How dare you! Pert chit! Look here, girl,' cried the old woman, shaking horribly with rage; 'if another word is said to me about money, I'll go and take apartments somewhere else.'

'Lady Teigne! You are ill,' cried Claire, as the old

woman sank back on her pillow, looking horribly purple.
'Let me send for a doctor.'

'What!' cried the old woman, springing up—'a doctor?
Don't you mention a doctor again in my presence, miss.
Do you think I'd trust myself to one of the villains? He'd
kill me in a week. Go and get my beef-tea. I'm quite
well.'

Claire went softly out of the room, and the old woman
sat up coughing and muttering.

'Worrying me for money, indeed—a dipperty-dapperty
dancing-master! I won't pay him a penny.'

Here there was a fit of coughing that made the fringe
dance till the old woman recovered, wiped her eyes, and
shook her skinny hand at the fringe for quivering.

'Doctor? Yes, they'd better. What do I want with a
doctor? Let them get one for old Lyddy—wants one worse
than I do, ever so much. Oh, there you are, miss. Is that
beef-tea strong?'

'Yes, Lady Teigne, very strong.'

Claire placed a tray, covered with a white napkin, before
her, and took the cover from the white china soup-basin,
beside which was a plate of toast cut up into dice.

The old woman sniffed at a spoonful.

'How much cognac did you put in?'

'A full wine-glass, Lady Teigne.'

'Then it's poor brandy.'

'No, Lady Teigne ; it is the best French.'

'Chut! Don't talk to me, child. I know what brandy is.'

She threw some of the sippets in, and began tasting the broth in an unpleasant way, mumbling between the spoonfuls.

'I knew what brandy was before you were born, and shall go on drinking it after you are dead, I dare say. There, I shan't have any more. Give it to that hungry boy of yours. He looks as if he wanted it.'

Claire could not forbear a smile, for the old woman had not left half a dozen spoonfuls at the bottom of the basin.

'Look here. Come up at two o'clock and dress me. I shall have a good many visitors to-day, and mind this: don't you ever hint at sending up Eliza again, or I'll go and take apartments somewhere else. We're getting proud, I suppose?'

There was a jingle of the china on the tray as the old woman threw herself down, and then a mumbling, followed by a fit of coughing, which soon subsided, and lastly there was nothing visible but the great cap-border, and a few straggling white hairs.

At two o'clock to the moment Claire went upstairs again, and for the space of an hour she performed the duties of lady's-maid without a murmur, building up the old relic of a bygone fashionable generation into a presentable form.

There was an auburn set of curls upon her head, with a huge tortoise-shell comb behind. A change had been wrought in her mouth, which was filled with white teeth. A thick coating of powder filled up some of her wrinkles, and a wonderful arrangement of rich lace draped her form as she sat propped up in an easy chair.

'Now my diamonds,' she said, at last; and Claire fetched a casket from the dressing-table, and held a mirror before the old lady, as she wearied herself—poor old flickering flame that she was!—fitting rings on her thin fingers, the glittering necklet about her baggy throat, the diadem in her hair, and the eardrops in the two yellow pendulous adjuncts to her head.

'Shall I do, chit?' she said, at last.

'Yes,' said Claire gravely.

'Humph! You don't look pleased; you never do. You're jealous, chit. There, half draw down the blinds and go, now. Leave the room tidy. I hate to have you by me at times like this.'

Claire helped her to walk to the drawing-room, arranged a few things, and then left the room with the folding doors closed, and it seemed as if life and youth had gone out of the place, leaving it to ghastly old age and death, painted with red lips and white cheeks, and looking ten times more awful than death in its natural solemn state.

Then for two hours fashionable Saltinville rattled the

knocker, and was shown up by Isaac, in ones, and twos, and
threes, and told Lady Teigne that she never looked better,
and took snuff, and gossiped, and told of the latest scandals
about Miss A., and Mr. B., and Lord C., and then stopped,
for Lord C. came and told tales back; and all the while
Lady Teigne, supported by Lady Drelincourt, her sister,
ogled and smiled, and smirked under her paint and diamonds, and quarrelled with her sister every time they were
left for a few minutes alone.

'It's shameful, Lyddy,' said her ladyship, pinching her
over-dressed sister; 'an old thing like you, rolling in riches,
and you won't pay my debts.'

'Pay them yourself,' was the ungracious reply.   'Oh!'

This was consequent upon the receipt of a severe pinch
from Lady Teigne, but the elderly sisters smiled again
directly, for Isaac announced Major Rockley, and the handsome, dark officer came in, banging an imaginary sabre at
his heels and clinking his spurs.   He kissed Lady Teigne's
hand, bent courteously over Lady Drelincourt, and then set
both tittering over the latest story about the Prince.

The sisters might have been young from their ways and
looks, and general behaviour towards the Major, whose
attentions towards the venerable animated mummy upon
the couch seemed marked by a manner that was almost
filial.

He patted the cushions that supported the weak back;

held her ladyship when a fit of coughing came on, and then had to find the necklet that had become unfastened and had slipped down beneath an Indian shawl, spread coverlet fashion, over the lady's trembling limbs.

'Thank you so much, Major. How clever you are!' cackled the old woman playfully, as he found the necklet, and clasped it about her throat. 'I almost feel disposed to give you some encouragement, only it would make Lyddy furious.'

Lady Drelincourt said 'For shame!' and tapped her sister with her fan, and then Major Rockley had to give place to Captain Bray and Lieutenant Sir Harry Payne, officers in his regiment, the former a handsome, portly dandy who puzzled his dearest friends, he was so poor but looked so well.

Then followed other members of the fashionable world of Saltinville, till nearly six, when the knocker ceased making the passage echo, the last visitor had called, and Claire helped —half carried—her ladyship back to bed, and watched her relock her jewels in the casket, which was taken then to the dressing-table. Her ladyship was made comfortable, partook of her dinner and tea, and then waited for the coming of Claire for the last time that night.

CHAPTER IV.

CLOUDS.

LADY TEIGNE's drawing-room was in full progress, and Claire was working hard at her tambour frame, earning money respectably, and listening to the coming and going of the visitors, when there was a tap at her bedroom door, and the maid Eliza entered.

'If you please, miss,' said Eliza, and stopped.

'Yes, Eliza,' and the soft white hand remained suspended over the canvas, with the needle glittering between the taper fingers.

'If you please, miss, there's that young man at the kitchen door.'

'That young man?'

'The soldier, miss; and he do look nice: Mr. James Bell.'

There was a flush in Eliza's face. It might have been that which fled from Claire's, leaving it like ivory.

'Where is your master?'

'He went out on the parade, miss.'

'And Mr. Morton?'

'Hush, miss! he said I wasn't to tell. He bought two herrings of Fisherman Dick at the back door, and I believe he've gone to the end of the pier, fishing.'

'I'll come down, Eliza.'

Eliza tripped off to hurry down to the handsome young dragoon waiting in the kitchen, and wonder whether he was Miss Claire's sweetheart, and wish he were hers, for he did look so lovely in his uniform and spurs.

As soon as Claire was alone she threw herself upon her knees beside her bed, to rise up at the end of a minute, the tears in her eyes, and a troubled look covering her handsome face with gloom.

Then she hurried down, barely escaping Major Rockley, who did contrive to raise his hat and direct a smile at her before she was gone—darting in at the empty breakfast-room door, and waiting there trembling till the Major had passed the window and looked up in vain to see if she were there.

'What a coincidence,' she thought, as her heart beat painfully, and a smarting blush came in her cheeks.

But the Major was gone; there was no fear of encountering him now; and she hurried into the kitchen, where a handsome, bluff-looking, fair young man of goodly proportions, who sat stiffly upright in his dragoon undress uniform, was talking to Eliza, who moved from the table against which she had been leaning, and left the kitchen.

'Oh, Fred dear,' cried Claire, as the blond young soldier rose from his chair, took her in his arms, and kissed her tenderly.

'Why, Claire, my pet, how are you?' he cried; and Eliza, who had peeped through the key-hole, gave her foot a spiteful stamp.

'So miserable, Fred dear. But you must not come here.'

'Oh, I won't come to the front, and disgrace you all; but hang it, you might let me come to the back. Getting too proud, I suppose.'

'Fred! don't talk so, dear. You hurt me.'

'Well, I won't, pet. Bless you for a dear, sweet girl. But it does seem hard.'

'Then why not try and leave the service, Fred? I'll save all I can to try and buy you out, but you must help me.'

'Bah! Stuff, little one! What's the good? Suppose I get my discharge, what's the good? What can I do? I shall only take to the drink again. I'm not fit for anything but a common soldier. No; I must stop as I am. The poor old governor meant well, Clairy, but it was beggarly work—flunkey work, and it disgusted me.'

'Oh, Fred!'

'Well, it did, little one. I was sick of the fashionable

starvation, and I suppose I was too fond of the drink, and so I enlisted.'

'But you don't drink much now, Fred.'

'Don't get the chance, little one,' he said, with a bluff laugh. 'There, I'll keep away. I won't disgrace you all.'

'Dear Fred,' said Claire, crying softly.

'And I won't talk bitterly to you, my pet. I say, didn't I see the Major come in at the front?'

'Yes, dear. He went up to see Lady Teigne. She is at home this afternoon.'

'Oh, that's right. Didn't come to see you. Master comes in at the front to see the countess; Private James Bell comes in at the back to see you, eh?'

'Fred, dear, you hurt me when you talk like this.'

'Then I'll be serious. Rum thing I should drift into being the Major's servant, isn't it? Makes me know him, though. I say, Clairy, you're a beautiful girl, and there's no knowing who may come courting.'

'Hush, Fred!'

'Not I. Let me speak. Look here: our Major's one of the handsomest men in the town, Prince's favourite, and all that sort of thing; but if ever he speaks to you, be on your guard, for he's as big a scoundrel as ever breathed, and over head in debt.'

'Don't be afraid, Fred,' said the girl, smiling.

'I'm not, pet. So the old girl's at home, is she?'

'Yes.'

'Sitting in her diamonds and lace, eh?'

Claire nodded.

'Wish I had some of them instead of that old cat—hang her!—for I'm awfully short of money. I say, dear, can you let me have a few shillings?'

Claire's white forehead wrinkled, and she looked at the young soldier in a troubled way, as she drew a little bead purse from her pocket, opened it, and poured five shillings into the broad hand.

'Thank ye,' he said coolly, as his eyes rested on the purse. Then, starting up—'Hang it, no,' he cried; 'I can't. Here, catch hold. Good-bye; God bless you!'

He thrust the money back into her hand, caught her in his arms and kissed her, and before she could detain him he was gone.

That afternoon and evening passed gloomily for Claire. Her father, when he returned from his walk, was restless and strange, and was constantly walking up and down the room.

To make matters worse, her visitor of that afternoon went by two or three times on the other side of the road, gazing very attentively up at the house, and she was afraid that their father might see him.

Then Major Rockley went by, smoking a cigar, raised his hat to her as he saw her at the window, and at the same moment as she returned his salute she saw Private James Bell on the other side, looking at her with a frown full of reproach.

Bedtime came at last, after a serious encounter between the Master of the Ceremonies and his son Morton for staying out till ten. Claire had to go to Lady Teigne again to give her the sleeping-draught she always took, eighty years not having made her so weary that she could sleep ; and then there was the wine-glass to half fill with water, and quite fill with salad oil, so that a floating wick might burn till morning.

' Good-night, Lady Teigne,' said Claire softly.

There was no answer ; and the young girl bent over the wreck of the fashionable beauty, thinking how like she ooked to death.

Midnight, and the tide going out, while the waves broke restlessly upon the shingle, which they bathed with pallid golden foam. The sea was black as ink, with diamonds sparkling in it here and there reflected from the encrusted sky ; and there was the glitter and sparkle of jewels in Lady Teigne's bedchamber, as two white hands softly lifted them from the wrenched-open casket.

That floating wick in the glass of oil looked like the condensation of some of the phosphorescence of the sea, and in its light the jewels glittered ; but it cast as well a boldly-thrown aquiline shadow on the chamber wall.

Ching!

The jewels fell back into the casket as a gasp came from the bed, and the man saw the light of recognition in the eyes that glared in his as the old woman sat up, holding herself there with her supporting hands.

' Ah !' she cried. ' You ?'

The word ' Help !'—a harsh, wild cry—was half formed, but only half, for in an instant she was dashed back, and the great down pillow pressed over her face.

The tide was going out fast.

CHAPTER V.

THERE was a flush on Claire Denville's cheek as she turned restlessly upon her pillow. Her dreams were of pain and trouble, and from time to time a sigh escaped her lips.

The rushlight which burned in a socket set in the middle of a tin cup of water, surrounded by a japanned cylinder full of holes, sent curious shadows and feeble rays about the plainly furnished room, giving everything a weird and ghostly look as the thin rush candle burned slowly down.

All at once she started up, listened, and remained there, hardly breathing. Then, as if not satisfied, she rose, hurriedly dressed herself, and, lighting a candle, went down to Lady Teigne's room.

The position had been unsought, but had been forced upon her by the exacting old woman, and by degrees Claire had found herself personal attendant, and liable to be called up at any moment during one of the many little attacks

that the great sapper and miner made upon the weak
fortress, tottering to its fall.

Was it fancy, or had she heard Lady Teigne
call?

It seemed to Claire, as she descended, that she had been
lying in an oppressive dream, listening to call after call, but
unable to move and master the unseen force that held her
down.

She paused as she reached the landing, with the drawing-
room door on her right, Lady Teigne's bedroom before her,
and, down a short passage on her left, her father's room.
Isaac slept in his pantry, by the empty plate-chest and the
wineless cellar. Morton's room was next her own, on the
upper floor, and the maids slept at the back.

The only sound to be heard was the faint wash of the
waves as they curled over upon the shingle where the tide
was going out.

'It must have been fancy,' said Claire, after listening
intently; and she stood there with the light throwing up
the eager look upon her face, with her lips half parted, and
a tremulous motion about her well-cut nostrils as her bosom
rose and fell.

Then, drawing a breath full of relief, she turned to go,
the horror that had assailed her dying off; for ever since
Lady Teigne had been beneath their roof, Claire had been
haunted by the idea that some night she would be called up

at a time when the visit her ladyship insisted in every act
was so far off had been paid.

Feeling for the moment, then, satisfied that she had been
deceived, Claire ascended three or four stairs, her sweet
face growing composed, and the soft, rather saddened smile
that generally sat upon her lips gradually returning, when,
as if moved by a fresh impulse, she descended again, listened, and then softly turned the handle of the door, and
entered.

She did not close the door behind her, only letting it swing
to, and then, raising the candle above her head, glanced
round.

There was nothing to take her attention.

The curtain of the bed was drawn along by the head, and
in an untidy way, leaving the end of the bolster exposed.
But that only indicated that the fidgety, querulous old
woman had fancied she could feel a draught from the folding
doors that led into the drawing-room, and she had often
drawn them like that before.

'She is fast asleep,' thought Claire.

The girl was right; Lady Teigne was fast asleep.

'If I let the light fall upon her face it will wake her,' she
said to herself.

But it was an error; the light Claire Denville carried was
too dim for that. Still she hesitated to approach the bedside, knowing that unless she took her opiate medicine Lady

Teigne's night's rest was of a kind that rendered her peevish and irritable the whole of the next day, and as full of whims as some fretful child

She seemed to be sleeping so peacefully that Claire once more glanced round the room prior to returning to bed.

The folding-doors were closed so that there could be no draught. The glass of lemonade was on the little table on the other side of the bed, on which ticked the little old carriage clock, for Lady Teigne was always anxious about the lapse of time. The jewel-casket was on the——

No : the jewel-casket was not on the dressing-table, and with a spasm of dread shooting through her, Claire Denville stepped quietly to the bedside, drew back the curtain, holding the candle above her head, let fall the curtain and staggered back with her eyes staring with horror, her lips apart, and her breath held for a few moments, but to come again with a hoarse sob.

She did not shriek aloud ; she did not faint. She stood there with her face thrust forward, her right arm crooked and extended as if in the act of drawing back the curtain, and her left hand still holding the candlestick above her head —stiffened as it were by horror into the position, and gazing still toward the bed.

That hoarse sob, that harsh expiration of the breath seemed to give her back her power of movement, and, turning swiftly, she ran from the room and down the short passage to rap quickly at her father's door.

'Papa! Papa!' she cried, in a hoarse whisper, trembling now in every limb, and gazing with horror-stricken face over her shoulder, as if she felt that she was being pursued.

Almost directly she heard a faint clattering sound of a glass rattling on the top of the water-bottle as someone crossed the room, the night-bolt was raised, the door opened, and the Master of the Ceremonies stood there, tall and thin, with his white hands tightly holding his long dressing-gown across his chest.

His face was ghastly as he gazed at Claire. There was a thick dew over his forehead, so dense that it glistened in the light of the candle, and made his grey hair cling to his white temples.

He had evidently not been undressed, for his stiff white cravat was still about his neck, and the silken strings of his pantaloons were still tied at the ankles. Moreover, the large signet-ring that had grown too large for his thin finger had not been taken off. It was as if he had hastily thrown off his coat, and put on his dressing-gown; but, though the night was warm, he was shivering, his lower lip trembling, and he had hard work to keep his teeth from chattering together like the glass upon the carafe.

'Father,' cried Claire, catching him by the breast, 'then you have heard something?'

'Heard—heard something?' he stammered; and then, seeming to make an effort to recover his *sang froid*, 'heard something? Yes—you—startled me.'

'But—but—oh, papa! It is too horrible!'

She staggered, and had to hold by him to save herself from falling. But recovering somewhat, she held him by one hand, then thrust herself away, looking the trembling man wildly in the face.

'Did you not hear—that cry?'

'No,' he said hastily, 'no. What is the matter?'

'Lady Teigne! Quick! Oh, father, it cannot be true!'

'Lady—Lady Teigne?' he stammered, 'is—is she—is she ill?'

'She is dead—she is dead!' wailed Claire.

'No, no! No, no! Impossible!' cried the old man, who was shivering visibly.

'It is true,' said Claire. 'No, no, it cannot be. I must be wrong. Quick! It may be some terrible fit!'

She clung to his hand, and tried to hurry him out of the room, but he drew back.

'No,' he stammered, 'not yet. Your—your news—agitated me, Claire. Does—wait a minute—does anyone—in the—in the house know?'

'No, dear. I thought I heard a cry, and I came down, and she——'

'A fit,' he said hastily, as he took the glass from the top

of the water-bottle, filled it, gulped the water down, and set bottle and glass back in their places. ' A fit—yes—a fit.'

' Come with me, father, quick !' cried Claire.

' Yes. Yes, I'll go with you—directly,' he said, fumbling for his handkerchief in the tail of the coat thrown over the chair, finding his snuff-box, and taking a great pinch.

' Come, pray come !' she cried again, as she gazed at him in a bewildered way, his trembling becoming contagious, and her lips quivering with a new dread greater than the horror at the end of the passage.

' Yes—yes,' he faltered—' I'll come. So alarming to be woke up—like this—in the middle of the night. Shall I— shall I ring, Claire ?   Or will you call the maids ?'

' Come with me first,' cried Claire.   ' It may not be too late.'

' Yes,' he cried, ' it is—it is too late.'

' Father !'

' You—you said she was dead,' he cried hastily.   ' Yes— yes—let us go.   Perhaps only a fit.   Come.'

He seemed to be now as eager to go as he had been to keep back, and, holding his child's hand tightly, he hurried with her to Lady Teigne's apartment, where he paused on the mat to draw a long, catching breath.

The next moment the door had swung to behind them, and father and daughter stood gazing one at the other.

'Don't, don't,' he cried, in a low, angry voice, as he turned from her. 'Don't look at me like that, Claire. What —what do you want me to do?'

Claire turned her eyes from him to gaze straight before her in a curiously dazed manner; and then, without a word, she crossed to the bedside and drew back the curtain, fixing her father with her eyes once more.

'Look!' she said, in a harsh whisper; 'quick! See whether we are in time.'

The old man uttered a curious supplicating cry, as if in remonstrance against the command that forced him to act, and, as if in his sleep, and with his eyes fixed upon those of his child, he walked up close to the bed, bent over it a moment, and then with a shudder he snatched the curtain from Claire's hand, and thrust it down.

'Dead!' he said, with a gasp. 'Dead!'

There was an awful silence in the room for a few moments, during which the ticking of the little clock on the table beyond the bed sounded painfully loud, and the beat of the waves amid the shingle rose into a loud roar.

'Father, she has been——'

'Hush!' he half shrieked, 'don't say so. Oh, my child, my child!'

Claire trembled, and it was as though a mutual attraction drew them to gaze fixedly the one at the other, in spite of every effort to tear their eyes away.

At last, with a wrench, the old man turned his head aside, and Claire uttered a low moan as she glanced from him to the bed and then back towards the window.

'Ah!' she cried, starting forward, and, bending down beside the dressing-table, she picked up the casket that was lying half hidden by drapery upon the floor.

But the jewel casket was quite empty, and she set it down upon the table. It had been wrenched open with a chisel or knife-blade, and the loops of the lock had been torn out.

'Shall we—a doctor—the constables?' he stammered.

'I—I do not know,' said Claire hoarsely, acting like one in a dream; and she staggered forward, kicking against something that had fallen near the casket.

She involuntarily stooped to pick it up, but it had been jerked by her foot nearer to her father, who bent down with the quickness of a boy and snatched it up, hiding it hastily beneath his dressing-gown, but not so quickly that Claire could not see that it was a great clasp-knife.

'What is that?' she cried sharply.

'Nothing—nothing,' he said.

They stood gazing at each other for a few moments, and then the old man uttered a hoarse gasp.

'Did—did you see what I picked up?' he whispered; and he caught her arm with his trembling hand.

'Yes; it was a knife.'

'No,' he cried wildly. 'No; you saw nothing. You did not see me pick up that knife.'

'I did, father,' said Claire, shrinking from him with an invincible repugnance.

'You did not,' he whispered. 'You dare not say you did, when I say be silent.'

'Oh, father! father!' she cried with a burst of agony.

'It means life or death,' he whispered, grasping her arm so tightly that his fingers seemed to be turned to iron. 'Come,' he cried with more energy, 'hold the light.'

He crossed the room and opened the folding-doors, going straight into the drawing-room, when the roar of the surf upon the shore grew louder, and as Claire involuntarily followed, she listened in a heavy-dazed way as her father pointed out that a chair had been overturned, and that the window was open and one of the flower-pots in the balcony upset.

'The jasmine is torn away from the post and balustrade,' he said huskily; 'someone must have climbed up there.'

Claire did not speak, but listened to him as he grew more animated now, and talked quickly.

'Let us call up Isaac and Morton,' he said. 'We must have help. The doctor should be fetched, and—and a constable.'

Claire gazed at him wildly.

'Did—did you hear anything?' he said hurriedly, as he closed the folding-doors.

'I was asleep,' said Claire, starting and shuddering as she heard his words. 'I thought I heard a cry.'

'Yes, a cry,' he said; 'I thought I heard a cry and I dressed quickly and was going to see, when—when you came to me. Recollect that you will be called up to speak, my child—an inquest—that is all you know. You went in and found Lady Teigne dead, and you came and summoned me. That is all you know.'

She did not answer, and he once more gripped her fiercely by the wrist.

'Do you hear me?' he cried. 'I say that is all you know.'

She looked at him again without answering, and he left her to go and summon Morton and the footman.

Claire stood in the drawing-room, still holding the candle-stick in her hand, with the stiffening form of the solitary old woman, whose flame of life had been flickering so weakly in its worldly old socket that the momentary touch of the extinguisher had been sufficient to put it out, lying just beyond those doors; on the other hand the roar of the falling tide faintly heard now through the closed window. She heard her father knocking at the door of her brother's room. Then she heard the stairs creak as he descended to call up the footman from the pantry below; and as she listened everything seemed strange and unreal, and she could not believe that a horror had fallen upon them that should make a hideous gulf between her and her father for ever, blast her young life so that she would never dare again to give her innocent love to the man by whom she knew she was idolised, and make her whole future a terror—a terror lest that which she felt she knew must be discovered, if she, weak woman that she was, ever inadvertently spoke what was life and light to her—the truth.

‘My God! What shall I do?’

It was a wild passionate cry for help where she felt that help could only be, and then, with her brain swimming, and a horrible dread upon her, she was about to open her lips and denounce her own father—the man who gave her life— as a murderer and robber of the dead. She turned to the door as it opened, and, deadly pale, but calm and firm now, Stuart Denville, Master of the Ceremonies at Saltinville, entered the room.

He uttered a low cry, and started forward to save her, but he was too late. Claire had fallen heavily upon her face, her hands outstretched, and the china candlestick she still held was shattered to fragments upon the floor.

At that moment, as if in mockery, a sweet, low chord of music rose from without, below the window, and floating away on the soft night air, the old man felt the sweet melody thrill his very nerves as he sank upon his knees beside his child.

CHAPTER VI.

A GHASTLY SERENADE.

'GENTLEMEN,' said Colonel Lascelles, 'I am an old fogey, and I never break my rules. At my time of life a man wants plenty of sleep, so I must ask you to excuse me. Rockley shall take my place, and I beg—I insist—that none will stir. Smith, send the Major's servant to see if he is better.'

A smart-looking dragoon, who had been acting the part of butler at the mess table, saluted.

'Beg pardon, sir, James Bell is sick.'

'Drunk, you mean, sir,' cried the Colonel angrily. 'Confound the fellow! he is always tippling the mess wine.'

'Small blame to him, Colonel,' said the Adjutant with tipsy gravity; ''tis very good.'

'And disagreed with his master early in the evening,' said the Doctor.

Here there was a roar of laughter, in which the grey-headed Colonel joined.

'Well, gentlemen, we must not be hard,' he said. 'Here, Smith, my compliments to Major Rockley, and if he is better, say we shall be glad to see him.'

'Beg pardon, sir,' said the man, 'here is the Major.'

At that moment the gentleman in question entered the room, and the brilliant illumination of the table gave a far better opportunity for judging his appearance than the blind-drawn gloom of Lady Teigne's drawing-room. He was a strikingly handsome dark man, with a fierce black moustache that seemed to divide his face in half, and then stood out beyond each cheek in a black tuft, hair highly pomatumed and curled, and bright black eyes that seemed to flash from beneath his rather overhanging brows. Five-and-thirty was about his age, and he looked it all, time or dissipation having drawn a good many fine lines, like tracings of future wrinkles, about the corners of his eyes and mouth.

'Colonel—gentlemen, a hundred apologies,' he said. 'I'm not often taken like this. We must have a fresh mess-man. Our cooking is execrable.'

'And your digestion so weak,' said the Doctor, sipping his port.

'There, there,' said the Colonel hastily. 'I want to get to bed. Take my place, Rockley; keep them alive. Good-night, gentlemen; I know you'll excuse me. Good-night.'

The Colonel left his seat, faced round, stood very stiffly

for a few moments, and then walked straight out of the room, while Major Rockley, who was still far from sober, took his place.

A good many bottles of port had been consumed that night, for in those days it was an English gentleman's duty to pay attention to his port, and after turning exceedingly poorly, and having to quit the table, the Major began by trying to make up for the past in a manner that would now be classed as loud.

'Gentlemen, pray—pray, pass the decanters,' he cried. 'Colonel Mellersh, that port is not to your liking. Smith, some more claret? Mr. Linnell, 'pon honour, you know you must not pass the decanter without filling your glass. Really, gentlemen, I am afraid our guests are disappointed at the absence of Colonel Lascelles, and because a certain gentleman has not honoured us to-night. A toast, gentlemen: H.R.H.'

'H.R.H.' was chorused as every officer and guest rose at the dark, highly-polished mahogany table, liberally garnished with decanters, bottles, and fruit; and, with a good deal of demonstration, glasses were waved in the air, a quantity of rich port was spilled, and the fact was made very evident that several of the company had had more than would leave them bright and clear in the morning.

The mess-room of the Light Dragoon Regiment was handsome and spacious; several trophies of arms and colours

decorated the walls; that unusual military addition, a con-
servatory, opened out of one side; and in it, amongst the
flowers, the music-stands of the excellent band that had
been playing during dinner were still visible, though the
bandsmen had departed when the cloth was drawn.

The party consisted of five-and-twenty, many being in
uniform, with their open blue jackets displaying their scarlet
dress vests with the ridge of pill-sized buttons closely packed
from chin to waist; and several of the wearers of these scarlet
vests were from time to time pouring confidences into their
neighbours' ears, the themes being two: 'The cards' and
'She.'

'Colonel Mellersh, I am going to ask you to sing,' said
Major Rockley, after taking a glass of port at a draught,
and looking a little less pale.

He turned to a striking-looking personage at his right
—a keen, aquiline-featured man, with closely-cut, iron-grey
hair, decisive, largish mouth with very white teeth, and
piercing dark grey eyes which had rather a sinister look
from the peculiarity of his fierce eyebrows, which seemed to
go upwards from where they nearly joined.

'I'm afraid my voice is in no singing trim,' said the
Colonel, in a quick, loud manner.

'Come, no excuses,' cried a big heavy-faced, youngish
man from the bottom of the long table—a gentleman already
introduced to the reader in Lady Teigne's drawing-room.

4—2

'No excuse, Sir Matt,' cried the Colonel; 'only an apology for the quality of what I am about to sing.'

There was a loud tapping and clinking of glasses, and then the Colonel trolled forth in a sweet tenor voice an anacreontic song about women, and sparkling wine, and eyes divine, and flowing bowls, and joyous souls, and ladies bright, as dark as night, and ladies rare, as bright as fair, and so on, and so on, the whole being listened to with the deepest attention and the greatest of satisfaction by a body of gentlemen whose thoughts at the moment, if not set upon women and wine, certainly were upon wine and women.

It was curious to watch the effect of the song upon the occupants of the different chairs. The Major sat back slightly flushed, gazing straight before him at the bright face he conjured up; Sir Matthew Bray leaned forward, and bent and swayed his great handsome Roman-looking head and broad shoulders in solemn satisfaction, and his nearest neighbour, Sir Harry Payne, the handsome, effeminate and dissipated young dragoon, tapped the table with his delicate fingers and showed his white teeth. The stout Adjutant bent his chin down over his scarlet waistcoat and stared fiercely at the ruby scintillations in the decanter before him. The gentleman on his left, an insignificant-looking little civilian with thin, fair hair, screwed up his eyes and drew up his lips in what might have been a smile or a sneer, and stared at the gentleman on the Major's left, holding himself a little sidewise so as to peer between one of the silver branches and the epergne.

The young man at whom he stared was worth a second look, as he leaned forward with his elbows upon the table and his head on one side, his cheek leaning upon his clasped hands.

He was fair with closely curling hair, broad forehead, dark eyes, and what was very unusual in those days, his face was innocent of the touch of a razor, his nut-brown beard curling closely and giving him rather a peculiar appearance among the scented and closely-shaven dandies around.

As the song went on he kept his eyes fixed on Colonel Mellersh, but the words had no charm for him: he was thinking of the man who sang, and of the remarkable qualities of his voice, uttering a sigh of satisfaction and sinking back in his seat as the song ended and there was an abundance of applause.

'Come,' cried Major Rockley, starting up again; 'I have done so well this time, gentlemen, that I shall call upon my friend here, Mr. Linnell, to give us the next song.'

'Indeed, I would with pleasure,' said the young man, colouring slightly; 'but Colonel Mellersh there will tell you I never sing.'

'No; Linnell never sings, but he's a regular Orpheus with his lute or pipe—I mean the fiddle and the flute.'

'Then perhaps he will charm us, and fancy he has come
into the infernal regions for the nonce; only, 'fore gad,
gentlemen, I am not the Pluto who has carried off his
Eurydice.'

'Really, this is so unexpected,' said the young man, 'and
I have no instrument.'

'Oh, some of your bandsmen have stringed instruments,
Rockley.'

'Yes, yes, of course,' cried the Major. 'What is it to be,
Mr. Linnell? We can give you anything. Why not get
up a quintette, and let Matt Bray there take the drum, and
charming Sir Harry Payne the cymbals?'

'Play something, Dick,' said Colonel Mellersh quietly.

'Yes, of course,' said the young man. 'Will you help
me?'

'Oh, if you like,' said the Colonel. 'Rockley, ask your
men to lend us a couple of instruments.'

'Really, my dear fellow, we haven't a lute in the regiment.'

'I suppose not,' said the Colonel dryly. 'A couple of
violins will do. Here, my man, ask for a violin and
viola.'

The military servant saluted and went out, and to fill up
the time Major Rockley proposed a toast.

'With bumpers, gentlemen. A toast that every man will
drink. Are you ready?'

There was a jingle of glasses, the gurgle of wine, and then a scattered volley of ' Yes!'

' Her bright eyes!' said the Major, closing his own and kissing his hand.

' Her bright eyes!' cried everyone but the Adjutant, who growled out a malediction on somebody's eyes.

Then the toast was drunk with three times three, there was the usual clattering of glasses as the gentlemen resumed their seats, and some of those who had paid most attention to the port began with tears in their eyes to expatiate on the charms of some special reigning beauty, receiving confidences of a like nature. Just then, the two instruments were brought and handed to the Colonel and Richard Linnell, a sneering titter going round the table, and a whisper about 'fiddlers' making the latter flush angrily.

' Yes, gentlemen, fiddlers,' said Colonel Mellersh quietly; ' and it requires no little skill to play so grand and old an instrument. I'll take my note from you, Dick.'

Flushing more deeply with annoyance, Richard Linnell drew his bow across the A string, bringing forth a sweet pure note that thrilled through the room, and made one of the glasses ring.

' That's right,' said the Colonel. ' I wish your father were here. What's it to be?'

' What you like,' said Linnell, whose eyes were wander-

ing about the table, as if in search of the man who would
dare to laugh and call him 'fiddler' again.

'Something simple that we know.'

Linnell nodded.

'Ready, gentlemen,' said the Major, with a sneering look
at Sir Harry Payne. 'Silence, please, ye demons of the
nether world. "Hark, the lute!" No: that's the wrong
quotation. Now, Colonel—Mr. Linnell, we are all attention.'

Richard Linnell felt as if he would have liked to box the
Major's ears with the back of the violin he held; but,
mastering his annoyance, he stood up, raised it to his
shoulder, and drew the bow across the strings, playing in
the most perfect time, and with the greatest expression, the
first bars of a sweet old duet, the soft mellow viola taking
up the seconds; and then, as the players forgot all present
in the sweet harmony they were producing, the notes came
pouring forth in trills, or sustained delicious, long-drawn
passages from two fine instruments, handled by a couple of
masters of their art.

As they played on sneers were changed for rapturous
admiration, and at last, as the final notes rang through the
room in a tremendous vibrating chord that it seemed could
never have been produced by those few tightly-drawn strings,
there was a furious burst of applause, glasses were broken,
decanters hammered the table, and four men who had sunk

beneath, suffering from too many bottles, roused up for the moment to shout ere they sank asleep again, while the Major excitedly stretched out his hand first to one and then to the other of the performers.

'Gentlemen,' he cried at last, hammering the table to obtain order, 'I am going to ask a favour of our talented guests. This has come upon me like a revelation. Such music is too good for men.'

'Hear! hear! hear! hear!' came in chorus.

'It is fit only for the ears of those we love.'

'Hear!—hear!—hear!—hear!'

'We have drunk their health, to-night; each the health of the woman of his heart.'

'Hear!—hear!—hear!—hear!'

'And now, as we have such music, I am going to beg our guests to come with us and serenade a lady whose name I will not mention.'

'Hear!—hear!—hurrah!'

'It is the lady I am proud to toast, and I ask the favour of you, Colonel Mellersh, of you, Mr. Linnell, to come and play that air once through beneath her window.'

'Oh, nonsense, Rockley. My dear fellow, no,' cried the Colonel.

'My dear Mellersh,' said the Major with half-tipsy gravity. 'My dear friend; and you, my dear friend Linnell, I pray you hear me. It may mean much more than you can tell—the happiness of my life   Come, my dear fellow, you'll not refuse.'

'What do you say, Linnell?' cried the Colonel good-humouredly.

'Oh, it is so absurd,' said Linnell warmly.

'No, no, not absurd,' said the Major sternly. 'I beg you'll not refuse.'

'Humour him, Dick,' said the Colonel in a whisper.

'You are telling him not to play,' said the Major fiercely.

'My dear fellow, no: I was asking him to consent. Humour him, Dick,' said the Colonel. 'It's nearly two, and there'll be no one about. If we refuse it may mean a quarrel.'

'I'll go if you wish it,' said Richard Linnell quietly.

'All right, Major; we'll serenade your lady in good old Spanish style,' said the Colonel laughingly. 'Quick, then, at once. How far is it?'

'Not far,' cried the Major. 'Who will come? Bray, Payne, and half a dozen more. Will you be one, Burnett?'

'No, not I,' said the little, fair man with the sneering smile; 'I shall stay;' and he gave effect to his words by sinking back in his chair and then gliding softly beneath the table.

'Just as you like,' said the Major, and the result was that a party of about a dozen sallied out of the barrack mess-room, crossed the yard, and were allowed to pass by the sentry on duty, carbine on arm.

It was a glorious night, and as they passed out into the fresh, pure air and came in sight of the golden-spangled sea, which broke amongst the shingle with a low, dull roar, the blood began to course more quickly through Linnell's veins, the folly of the adventure was forgotten, and a secret wish that he and the Colonel were alone and about to play some sweet love ditty, beneath a certain window, crossed his brain.

For there was something in the time there, beneath the stars that were glitteringly reflected in the sea! Did she love him? Would she ever love him? he thought, and he walked on in a sweet dream of those waking moments, forgetful of the Major, and hearing nothing of the conversation of his companions, knowing nothing but the fact that he was a man of seven and twenty, whose thoughts went hourly forth to dwell upon one on whom they had long been fixed, although no words had passed, and he had told himself too often that he dare not hope.

' Who is the Major's Gloriana, Dick?' asked the Colonel suddenly. ' By Jove, I think we had better tune up a jig. It would be far more suited to the woman he would choose than one of our young composer's lovely strains.'

' I don't know. He's going towards our place. Can it be Cora Dean?'

'Hang him, no,' said the Colonel pettishly. 'Perhaps so, though. I hope not, or we shall have your father calling us idiots—deservedly so—for our pains. Wrong, Dick; the old man will sleep in peace. Will it be Drelincourt?'

'Madame Pontardent, perhaps.'

'No, no, no, my lad; he's going straight along. How lovely the sea looks!'

'And how refreshing it is after that hot, noisy room.'

'Insufferable. What fools men are to sit and drink when they might play whist!'

'And win money,' said Linnell drily.

'To be sure, my lad. Oh, you'll come to it in time. Where the dickens is he going? Who can the lady be?'

The Major evidently knew, for he was walking smartly ahead, in earnest converse with half a dozen more. Then came the Colonel and his companion, and three more of the party brought up the rear.

The Major's course was still by the row of houses that faced the sea, now almost without a light visible, and Richard Linnell was dreamily watching the waves that looked like liquid gold as they rose, curved over and broke upon the shingle, when all the blood seemed to rush at once to his heart, and then ebb away, leaving him choking and paralyzed, for the Colonel suddenly said aloud:

'Claire Denville!'

And he saw that their host of the night had stopped before the house of the Master of the Ceremonies.

The blood began to flow again, this time with a big wave of passionate rage in Richard Linnell's breast. He was furious. How dared that handsome libertine profane Claire Denville by even thinking of her? How dared he bring him there, to play beneath the window—the window he had so often watched, and looked upon as a sacred temple—the resting-place of her he loved.

He was ready to seize the Major by the throat; to fight for her; to say anything; to dash down the instrument in his rage; to turn and flee; but the next moment the cool, calm voice of the Colonel brought him to his senses, and he recalled that this was his secret—his alone—this secret of his love.

' I did not know the Major was warm there. Well, she's a handsome girl, and he's welcome, I dare say.'

Linnell felt ready to choke again, but he could not speak. He must get out of this engagement, though, at any cost.

As he was musing, though, he found himself drawn as it were to where the Major and his friends were standing in front of the silent house, and the Colonel said :

' Come, my lad, let's run through the piece, and get home to bed. I'm too old for such tom-fool tricks as these.'

' I will not play! It is an insult! It is madness!' thought Richard Linnell; and then, as if in a dream, he found himself the centre of a group, fuming at what he was doing, while, as if in spite of his rage, he was drawing the sweet echoing strains from the violin, listening to the harmonies added by his friend, and all in a nightmare-like fashion, playing involuntarily on, and gazing at the windows he had so often watched.

On, on, on, the notes poured forth, throbbing on the night-air, sounding pensive, sweet and love-inspiring, maddening too, as he tried to check his thoughts, and played with more inspiration all the while till the last bar, with its diminuendo, was reached, and he stood there, palpitating, asking himself why he had done this thing, and waiting trembling in his jealous rage, lest any notice should be taken of the compliment thus paid.

Did Claire Denville encourage the Major—that libertine whose amours were one of the scandals of the place? Oh, it was impossible. She would not have heard the music. If she had she would have thought it from some wanderers, for she had never heard him play. She would not notice it. She would not heed it. In her virgin youth and innocency it was a profanation to imagine that Claire Denville—sweet, pure Claire Denville—the woman he worshipped, could notice such an attention. No, it was impossible she would; and his eyes almost started as he gazed at the white-curtained windows, looking so solemn and so strange.

No, no, no; she would not notice, even if she had heard,

nd a strange feeling of elation came into the jealous
breast.

'Come,' he said hoarsely, 'let us go.'

'One moment, lad. Ah, yes,' said the Colonel. 'Gloriana
has heard the serenade, and is about to respond to her lover's
musically amatory call. Look, Dick, look.'

Richard Linnell's heart sank, for a white arm drew back
the curtain, and then the catch of the window fastening was
pressed back, and a chord in the young man's breast seemed
to snap; but it was only the spring of the window hasp.

Click!

CHAPTER VII.

THE 'ghastly serenade' it was called at Saltinville as the facts became known.

That night Richard Linnell was standing with his teeth set, his throat dry, and a feeling of despair making his heart seem to sink, watching the white hand that was waved as soon as the sash was opened. Half blind with the blood that seemed to rush to his eyes, he glared at the window. Then a sudden revulsion of feeling came over him as a familiar voice that was not Claire's cried, 'Help!—a doctor!' and then the speaker seemed to stagger away.

The rest was to Richard Linnell like some dream of horror, regarding which he recalled the next morning that he had thundered at the door, that he had helped to carry Claire to her room, and that he had afterwards been one of the group who stood waiting in the dining-room until the doctor came down to announce that Miss Denville was better—that Lady Teigne was quite dead.

Then they had stolen out on tiptoe, and in the stillness of the early morning shaken hands all round and separated, the Major remaining with them, and walking with Colonel Mellersh and Richard Linnell to their door.

'What a horror!' he said hoarsely. 'I would not for the world have taken you two there had I known. Good-night —good-morning, I should say;' and he, too, said those words—perhaps originated the saying—'What a ghastly serenade !'

Nine days—they could spare no more in Saltinville, for it would have spoiled the season—nine days' wonder, and then the news that a certain royal person was coming down, news blown by the trumpet of Fame with her attendants, raised up enough wind to sweep away the memory of the horror on the Parade.

'She was eighty if she was a day,' said Sir Matthew Bray : 'and it was quite time the old wretch did die.'

'Nice way of speaking of a lady whose relative you are seeking to be,' said Sir Harry Payne. 'Sweet old nymph. How do you make it fit, Matt ?'

'Fit ? Some scoundrel of a London tramp scaled the balcony, they say. Fine plunder, the rascal ! All those diamonds.'

'Which she might have left her sister, and then perhaps they would have come to you, Matt.'

'Don't talk stuff.'

'Stuff? Why, you are besieging the belle. But, I say, I have my own theory about that murder.'

'Eh, have you?' cried the great dragoon, staring open-mouthed.

'Egad! yes, Matt. It was not a contemptible robbery.'

'Wasn't it? You don't say so.'

'But I do,' cried Sir Harry seriously. 'Case of serious jealousy on the part of some lover of the bewitching creature. He came i' the dead o' night and smothered the Desdemona with a pillow. What do you say, Rockley?'

The Major had strolled across the mess-room and heard these words.

'Bah! Don't ridicule the matter,' he said. 'Change the subject.'

'As you like, but the feeble flame only wanted a momentary touch of the extinguisher and it was gone.'

At the house on the Parade there had been terrible anguish, and Claire Denville suffered painfully as she passed through the ordeal of the examination that ensued.

But everything was very straightforward and plain. There were the marks of some one having climbed up the pillar—an easy enough task. The window opened without difficulty from without, a pot or two lay overturned in the balcony, a chair in the drawing-room, evidently the work of some stranger, and the valuable suite of diamonds was gone.

The constable arrested three men of the street tumbler

and wandering vagrant type, who were examined, proved easily that they were elsewhere; and after the vote of condolence to our esteemed fellow-townsman, Stuart Denville, Esq., which followed the inquest, there seemed nothing more to be done but to bury Lady Teigne, which was accordingly done, and the principal undertaker cleared a hundred pounds by the grand funeral that took place, though it was quite a year before Lady Drelincourt would pay the whole of his bill.

So with Lady Teigne the horror was buried too, and in a fortnight the event that at one time threatened to interfere with the shopkeepers' and lodging-letters' season was forgotten.

For that space of time, too, the familiar figure of the Master of the Ceremonies was not seen upon the Parade. Miss Denville was very ill, it was said, and after the funeral Isaac had to work hard at answering the door to receive the many cards that were left by fashionable people, till there was quite a heap in the old china bowl that stood in the narrow hall.

But the outside world knew nothing of the agonies of mind endured by the two principal occupants of that house —of the nights of sleepless horror passed by Claire as she knelt and prayed for guidance, and of the hours during which the Master of the Ceremonies sat alone, staring blankly before him as if at some scene which he was ever witnessing, and which seemed to wither him, mind and body, at one stroke.

For that fortnight, save at the inquest, father and daughter had not met, but passed their time in their rooms. But the time was gliding on, and they had to meet—the question occurring to each—how was it to be ?

'I must leave it to chance,' thought the Master of the Ceremonies, with a shiver; and after a fierce struggle to master the agony he felt, he knew that in future he must lead two lives. So putting on his mask, he one morning walked down to the breakfast-room, and took his accustomed place.

Outwardly he seemed perfectly calm, and, save that the lines about his temples and the corners of his lips seemed deeper, he was little changed ; but as he walked he was conscious of a tremulous feeling in the knees, and even when seated, that the curious palsied sensation went on.

On the previous night Morton had come in from a secret fishing excursion, to find the house dark and still, and he had stood with his hands in his pockets hesitating as to whether he should go and take a lesson in smoking with Isaac in the pantry, steal down to the beach, or creep upstairs.

He finally decided on the latter course, and going up to the top of the house on tip-toe, he tapped softly at Claire's bedroom door.

It was opened directly by his sister, who had evidently just risen from an old dimity-covered easy-chair. She was in a long white dressing-gown, and, seen by the light of the one tallow candle on the table, she looked so pale and ghastly that the lad uttered an ejaculation and caught hold of her thin, cold hands.

'Claire!—Sis!'

They were the first warm words of sympathy she had heard since that horrible night; and in a moment the icy horror upon her face broke up, her lips quivered, and, throwing her arms around her brother's neck, she burst into such a passion of hysterical sobbing that, as he held her to his breast, he grew alarmed.

He had stepped into the little white room where the flower screen stood out against the night sky, and as the door swung to, he had felt Claire sinking upon her knees, and imitating her action, he had held her there for some time till the attitude grew irksome, and then sank lower till he was seated on the carpet, holding his sister half-reclining across his breast.

'Oh! don't—don't, Claire—Sis,' he whispered from time to time, as he kissed the quivering lips, and strove in his boyish way to soothe her. 'Sis dear, you'll give yourself such a jolly headache. Oh, I say, what's the good of crying like that?'

For answer she only clung the tighter, the pent-up agony

escaping in her tears, though she kissed him passionately again and again, and nestled to his breast.

'You'll make yourself ill, you know,' he whispered. 'I say, don't. The dad's ill, and you'll upset him more.'

Still she sobbed on and wept, the outburst saving her from some more terrible mental strain.

'I wanted to come and comfort you,' he said. 'I did not know you'd go on like this.'

She could not tell him that he was comforting her; that she had been tossed by a horrible life-storm that threatened to wreck her reason, and that when she had lain longing for the sympathy of the sister who now kept away, saying it was too horrible to come there now, she had found no life-buoy to which to cling. And now her younger brother had come—the elder forbidden the house—and the intensity of the relief she felt was extreme.

'Here, I can't stand this,' he said at last, almost roughly. 'I shall go down and send Ike for the doctor.'

She clung to him in an agony of dread lest he should go, and her sobs grew less frequent.

'Come, that's better,' he said, and he went on in his rough boyish selfishness, talking of his troubles and ignoring those of others, unconsciously strengthening Claire, as he awakened her to a sense of the duties she owed him, and giving her mental force for the terrible meeting and struggle that was to come.

For she dared not think. She shrank from mentally arguing out those two questions of duty—to society and to her father.

Was she to speak and tell all she knew?

Was she to be silent?.

All she could do was to shrink within herself, and try to make everything pass out of her thoughts while she was sinking into the icy chains of idiocy.

But now, when she had been giving up completely, and at times gazing out to sea with horrible thoughts assailing her, and suggestions like temptations to seek for oblivion as the only escape from the agony she suffered, the life-raft had reached her hands, and she clung to it with all the tenacity of one mentally drowning fast.

There was something soothing in the very sound of her brother's rough voice speaking in a hoarse whisper; and his selfish repinings over the petty discomforts he had suffered came like words of comfort and rest.

' It has been so jolly blank and miserable downstairs,' he went on as he held her, and involuntarily rocked himself to and fro. 'Ike and Eliza have been always gossiping at the back and sneaking out to take dinner or tea or supper with somebody's servants, so as to palaver about what's gone on here.'

A pause.

'There's been scarcely anything to eat. I've been half starved.'

' Oh, Morton, my poor boy !'

Those were the first words Claire had uttered since the inquest, and they were followed by a fresh burst of sobs.

' Oh, come, come. Do leave off,' he cried pettishly. ' I say it's all very well for the old man to growl at me for fishing, but if I hadn't gone catching dabs and a little conger or two, I should have been starved.'

She raised her face and kissed him. Some one else was suffering, and her woman's instinct to help was beginning to work.

' What do you think I did, Sis? Oh, you don't know. I'd been up to Burnett's to see May, but the beggars had sneaked off and gone to London. Just like Franky Sneerums and wax doll May. Pretty sort of a sister to keep away when we're in trouble.'

' Oh, don't, my dear boy,' whispered Claire in a choking voice.

' Oh, yes, I shall. They're ashamed of me and of all of us. Just as if we could help the old girl being killed here.'

A horrible spasm ran through Claire.

' Don't jump like that, stupid,' said Morton roughly. ' You didn't kill her.'

' Hush ! hush !'

' No, I shan't hush. It'll do you good to talk and hear what people say, my pretty old darling Sis. There, there, hush-a-bye, baby. Cuddle up close, and let's comfort you. What's the matter now ?'

Claire had struggled up, with her hands upon his shoulders, and was gazing wildly into his eyes.

'What—what do people say ?' she panted.

'Be still, little goose—no ; pretty little white pigeon,' he said, more softly, as he tried to draw her towards him.

'What—do they say ?' she cried, in a hoarse whisper, and she trembled violently.

'Why, that it is a jolly good job the old woman is dead, for she was no use to anyone.'

Claire groaned as she yielded once more to his embrace.

'Fisherman Dick says—I say, he is a close old nut there's no getting anything out of him !—says he don't see that people like Lady Teigne are any use in the world.'

'Morton !'

'Oh, it's all right. I'm only telling you what he said. He says too that the chap who did it—— I say, don't kick out like that, Sis. Yes, I shall go on : I'm doing you good. Fisherman Dick, and Mrs. Miggles too, said that I ought to try and rouse you up, and I'm doing it. You're ever so much better already. Why, your hands were like dabs when I came up, and now they are nice and warm.'

She caressed his cheek with them, and he kissed her as she laid her head on his shoulder.

'Dick Miggles said that the diamonds would never do the chap any good who stole 'em.'

Once more that hysterical start, but the boy only clasped his sister more tightly, and went on :

'Dick says he never knew anyone prosper who robbed or murdered, or did anything wrong, except those who smuggled. I say, Sis, I do feel sometimes as if I should go in for a bit of smuggling. There are some rare games going on.'

Claire clung to him as if exhausted by her emotion.

'Dick's been in for lots of it, I know, only he's too close to speak. I don't know what I should have done if it hadn't been for them. I've taken the fish I've caught up there, and Polly Miggles has cooked them, and we've had regular feeds.'

'You have been up there, Morton ?' said Claire wildly.

'Yes ; you needn't tell the old man. What was I to do ? I couldn't get anything to eat here. I nursed the little girl for Mrs. Miggles while she cooked, and Dick has laughed at me to see me nurse the little thing, and said it was rum. But I don't mind ; she's a pretty little tit, and Dick has taught her to call me uncle.'

CHAPTER VIII.

THE FIRST MEETING.

It was the next morning that the Master of the Ceremonies made his effort, and went down to the breakfast-room, where he sat by the table, playing with the newspaper that he dared not try to read, and waiting, wondering, in a dazed way, whether his son or his daughter would come in to breakfast.

The paper fell from his hands, and as he sat there he caught at the table, drawing the cloth aside and holding it with a spasmodic clutch, as one who was in danger of falling.

For there was the creak of a stair, the faint rustle of a dress, and he knew that the time had come.

He tried to rise to his feet, but his limbs refused their office, and the palsied trembling that had attacked him rose to his hands. Then he loosened his hold of the table, and sank back in his chair, clinging to the arms, and with his chin falling upon his breast.

At that moment the door opened, and Claire glided into the room.

She took a couple of steps forward, after closing the door, and then caught at the back of a chair to support herself.

The agony and horror in his child's face, as their eyes met, galvanized Denville into life, and, starting up, he took a step forward, extending his trembling hands.

'Claire—my child!' he cried, in a husky voice.

His hands dropped, his jaw fell, his eyes seemed to be starting, as he read the look of horror, loathing, and shame in his daughter's face, and for the space of a full minute neither spoke.

Then, as if moved to make another effort, he started spasmodically forward.

'Claire, my child—if you only knew!'

But she shrank from him with the look of horror intensified.

'Don't—don't touch me,' she whispered, in a harsh, dry voice. 'Don't: pray don't.'

'But, Claire——'

'I know,' she whispered, trembling violently. 'It is our secret. I will not speak. Father—they should kill me first; but don't—don't. Father—father—you have broken my heart!'

As she burst forth in a piteous wail in these words, the

terrible involuntary shrinking he had seen in her passed away. The stiff angularity that had seemed to pervade her was gone, and she sank upon her knees, holding by the back of the chair, and rested her brow upon her hands, sobbing and drawing her breath painfully.

He stood there gazing down at her, but for a time he did not move. Then, taking a step forward, he saw that she heard him, and shrank again.

'Claire, my child,' he gasped once more, ' if you only knew !'

'Hush !—for God's sake, hush !' she said, in a whisper. ' Can you not see ? It is our secret. You are my father. I am trying so hard. But don't—don't——'

'Don't touch you !' he cried slowly, as she left her sentence unspoken. ' Well, be it so,' he added, with a piteous sigh ; ' I will not complain.'

'Let it be like some horrible dream,' she said, in the same low, painful whisper. ' Let me—let me go away.'

'No !' he cried, with a change coming over him ; and he drew himself up as if her words had given him a sudden strength. ' You must stay. You have duties here, and I have mine. Claire, you must stay, and it must be to you— to me, like some horrible dream. Some day you may learn the horrible temptations that beset my path. Till then I accept my fate, for I dare not confide more, even to you. Heaven help me in this horror, and give me strength !' he muttered to himself, with closed eyes. 'I dare not die; I cannot—I will not die. I must wear the mask. Two lives to live, when heretofore one only has been so hard!'

Just then there was a quick step outside, and the tall figure of Morton Denville passed the window.

The Master of the Ceremonies glanced at Claire, who started to her feet, and then their eyes met.

'For his sake, Claire,' he whispered, 'if not for mine.'

'For his sake—father,' she answered, slowly and reverently, as if it were a prayer; and then to herself, 'and for yours—the duty I owe you as your child.'

'And I,' he muttered to himself, as he stood with a white hand resting upon the table. 'I must bear it to the end. I must wear my mask as of old, and wilt Thou give me pardon and the strength?'

Morton entered the room fresh and animated, and his eyes lit up as he saw that it was occupied.

'That's better!' he cried. 'Morning, father,' and he clasped the old man's hand.

'Good-morning, my dear boy,' was the answer, in trembling tones; and then, with the ghost of a smile on the wan lips, 'have you been——'

Morton had boisterously clasped Claire in his arms, and kissed her with effusion; and as he saw the loving, wistful look in his child's face, as she passionately returned the caress—one that he told himself would never again be bestowed on him—a pang shot through the old man's breast, and the agony seemed greater than he could bear.

'So—so glad to see you down again, my dear, dear, dear old Sis,' cried Morton, with a kiss at almost every word. Then, half holding her still, he turned to the pale, wistful face at the other side of the room, and exclaimed :

'Yes, sir. Don't be angry with me. I *have* been down again, catching dabs.'

CHAPTER IX.

WEARING HIS MASK.

'REALLY, ladies, I—er—should—er—esteem it an honour, but my powers here are limited, and——'

'Rubbish!'

'You'll pardon me?'

'I say—rubbish, Denville.'

'Mamma, will you hold your tongue?'

'No, miss; if it comes to that, I won't! Speaking like that to your own mother, who's always working for you as I am, right out here on the open cliff, where goodness knows who mayn't——'

'Mother, be silent!'

'Silent, indeed!'

'Ladies, ladies, you'll pardon me. I say my powers here are—er—very limited.'

'Yes, I know all about that, but you must get invitations for mamma and me for the next Assembly.'

'I'll try, Miss Dean, but—you'll pardon me——'

'There, don't shilly-shally with him, Betsy; it's all business. Look here, Denville, the day the invitations come there'll be five guineas wrapped up in silver paper under the chayny shepherdess on my droring-room mantelpiece, if you'll just call and look under.'

'Really, Mrs. Dean, you—you shock me. I could not think of—er—really—er—I will try my best.'

'That you will, I know, Mr. Denville. Don't take any notice of mamma I hope Miss Denville and Mrs. Burnett are well.'

'In the best of health, Miss Dean, I thank you. I will—er—do my best. A lovely morning, Mrs. Dean. Your humble servant. Miss Cora, yours. Good-morning.'

'A nasty old humbug; but he'll have the invitations sent,' said Mrs. Dean, a big, well-developed, well-preserved woman of fifty, with bright dark eyes that glistened and shone like pebbles polished by the constant attrition of the blinking lids.

'I wish you would not be so horridly coarse, mother; and if you don't drop that "Betsy" we shall quarrel,' said the younger lady, who bore a sufficient likeness to the elder for anyone to have stamped them mother and daughter, though the latter was wanting in her parent's hardness of outline, being a magnificent specimen of womanly beauty. Dark and thoroughly classic of feature, large-eyed, full-lipped, perhaps rather too highly coloured, but this was carried off by the luxuriant black hair, worn in large ringlets flowing down either side of the rounded cheeks they half concealed, by her well-arched black brows and long dark lashes, which shaded her great swimming eyes. Her figure was perfect, and she was in full possession of the ripest womanly beauty, as she walked slowly and with haughty carriage along the cliff, beside the elder dame.

Both ladies were dressed in the very height of the fashion, with enormous wide-spreading open bonnets, heavy with ostrich plumes, tightly-fitting dresses, with broad waistbands well up under the arms, loose scarves, long gloves and reticules ornamented with huge bows of the stiffest silk, like Brobdingnagian butterflies.

'Horrid, coarse indeed! I suppose I mustn't open my mouth next,' said the elder lady.

'It would be just as well not,' said the younger, 'when we are out.'

'Then I shall open it as wide as I like, ma'am, and when I like, so now then, Betsy.'

'As you please ; only if you do, I shall go home, and I shall not go to Assembly or ball with you. It was your wish that I should be Cora.'

'No, it wasn't. I wanted Coral, or Coralie, miss.'

'And I preferred Cora,' said the younger lady with languid hauteur, as if she were practising a part, 'and you are always blurting out Betsy.'

'Blurting! There's a way to speak to your poor mother, who has made the lady of you that you are. Carriages and diamonds, and grand dinners, and——'

'The smell of the orange peel, and the candles, and the memory of the theatre tacked on to me. "Actress!" you can see every fine madam we pass say with her eyes, as she draws her skirt aside and turns from me as if I polluted the cliff. I've a deal to be proud of,' cried the younger woman fiercely. 'For heaven's sake, hold your tongue!'

'Don't go on like that, Betsy—Cora, I mean, my dear. Let 'em sneer. If your poor, dear, dead father did keep a show—well, there, don't bite me, Bet—Cora—*theatre*, and make his money, it's nothing to them, and you'll make a marriage yet, as'll surprise some of 'em if you plays your cards proper!'

'Mother!'

'Say mamma, my dear, now; and do smooth down, my beauty. There, there, there! I didn't mean to upset you. There's Lord Carboro coming. Don't let him see we've been quarrelling again. I don't know, though,' she added softly, as she noticed her child's heightened colour and heaving bosom; 'it do make you look so 'andsome, my dear.'

'Pish!'

'It do, really. What a beauty you are, Cora. I don't wonder at the fools going mad after you and toasting you—as may be a countess if you like.'

6—2

'Turn down here,' said Cora abruptly. 'I don't want to see Carboro.'

'But he made me a sign, my dear; with his eyeglass, dear.'

'Let him make a hundred,' cried Cora angrily. 'He is not going to play with me. Why, he's hanging about after that chit of Denville's.'

'Tchah! Cora dear. I wouldn't be jealous of a washed-out doll of a thing like that. Half-starved paupers; and with the disgrace of that horrid murder sticking all over their house.'

'Jealous!' cried Cora, with a contemptuous laugh; 'jealous of her! Not likely, mother; but I mean to make that old idiot smart if he thinks he is going to play fast and loose with me. Come along.'

Without noticing the approaching figure, she turned up the next street, veiling her beautiful eyes once more with their long lashes, and gliding over the pavement with her magnificent figure full of soft undulations that the grotesque fashion of the dress of the day could not hide.

'Oh, Cora, my darling,' said her mother, 'how can you be so mad and obstinate!—throwing away your chances like that.'

'Chances? What do you mean?' cried the beauty.

'Why, you know, my dear. He has never married yet; and he's so rich, and there's his title.'

' And are we so poor that we are to humble ourselves and beg because that man has a title ?'

' But it is such a title, Betsy,' whispered the elder woman.

' And he is so old, and withered, and gouty, and is obliged to drive himself out in a ridiculous donkey-chaise.'

' Now, what does that matter, dear ?'

' Not much to you, seemingly.'

' Now, my lovely, don't—don't. To think that I might live to see my gal, Betsy Dean, a real countess, and such a one as there ain't anywhere at court, and she flying in my face and turning her back upon her chances.'

' Mother, do you want to put me in a rage.'

' Not in the street, dear ; but do—do—turn back !'

' I shall not.'

' Then I know the reason why,' cried the elder woman.

' What do you mean ?'

' You're thinking of that nasty, poverty-stricken, brown-faced fiddler of a fellow, who hasn't even the decency to get himself shaved. I declare he looks more like a Jew than a Christian.'

' You mean to make me angry, mother.'

' I don't care if I do. There, I say it's a sin and a shame. A real Earl—a real live Lord as good as proposing to you, and you, you great silly soft goose, sighing and whining after a penniless pauper who won't even look at you. Oh ! the fools gals are !'

Cora Dean's lips were more scarlet than before, and her beautiful eyes flashed ominously, but she said nothing.

'Going silly after a fellow like that, who's for ever hanging about after Denville's gal. Oh! I hav'n't patience.'

She said no more, for her daughter walked so fast that she became short of breath.

'Egad! Juno's put out,' said James, Earl of Carboro, peer of the realm, speaking in a high-pitched voice, and then applying one glove to his very red lips, as if he were uneasy there. 'What a magnificent figure, though! She's devilish handsome, she is, egad! It's just as well, perhaps. I won't follow her. I'll go on the pier. Let her come round if she likes, and if she doesn't—why, demme, I don't care if she doesn't—now that——'

He smacked his lips, and shook his head, and then drew himself up, rearranging his quaint beaver hat that came down fore and aft, curled up tightly at the sides, and spread out widely at the flat top. He gave his ancient body a bit of a writhe, and then raised his gold eyeglass to gaze at the pier, towards which people seemed to be hastening.

'Eh? Egad, why, what's the matter? Somebody gone overboard? I'll go and see. No, I won't; I'll sit down and wait. I shall soon know. It's deuced hot. Those railings are not safe.'

He settled himself on the first seat on the cliff, and, giving the wide watered-silk ribbon a shake, used his broad and square gold-rimmed eyeglass once more, gazing through it at the long, old-fashioned pier that ran down into the sea, amongst whose piles the bright waves that washed the chalky shore of fashionable Saltinville were playing, while an unusual bustle was observable in the little crowd of loungers that clustered on the long low erection.

Meanwhile the Master of the Ceremonies of the fashionable seaside resort honoured of royalty had continued his course towards the pier.

The trouble at his house seemed to be forgotten, and in the pursuit of his profession to serve and be observed—gentleman-in-waiting on society—he looked to-day a tall, rather slight man, with nut-brown hair, carefully curled and slightly suggestive of having been grown elsewhere, closely shaven face of rather careworn aspect, but delicate and refined. He was a decidedly handsome, elderly man, made ridiculous by a mincing dancing-master deportment, an assumed simpering smile, and a costume in the highest fashion of George the Third's day. His hat has been already described, for it was evidently moulded on the same block as my Lord Carboro's, and the rest of the description will do for the costume of both—in fact, with allowances for varieties of colour and tint, for that of most of the gentlemen who flit in and out in the varied scenes of this story of old seaside life.

His thin, but shapely legs were in the tightest of pantaloons, over which were a glossy pair of Hessian boots with silken tassels where they met the knee.   An extremely tight tail coat of a dark bottle green was buttoned over his breast, leaving exposed a goodly portion of a buff waistcoat below the bottom buttons, while the coat collar rose up like a protecting erection, as high as the wearer's ears, and touched and threatened to tilt forward the curly brimmed hat.   Two tiny points of a shirt collar appeared above the sides of an enormous stock which rigidly prisoned the neck; a delicate projection of cambric frilling rose from the breast; the hands were tightly gloved, one holding a riding-whip, the top of which was furnished with a broad-rimmed square eyeglass; and beneath the buff vest hung, suspended by a broad, black watered-silk ribbon, a huge bunch of gold seals and keys, one of the former being an enormous three-tabled topaz, which turned in its setting at the wearer's will.

Such was the aspect of the Master of the Ceremonies in morning costume—the man whose services were sought by every new arrival for introduction to the Assembly Room and to the fashionable society of the day—the man who, by unwritten canons of the fashionable world, must needs be consulted for every important fête or dance, and whose offerings from supplicants—he scorned to call them clients —were supposed to yield him a goodly income, and doubtless would do so, did the season happen to be long, and society at Saltinville in force.

Parting from the ladies he had met, he passed on with a feeble smirk, growing more decided, his step more mincing, to bow to some lady, a proceeding calling for grace and ease. The raising and replacing of the hat was ever elaborate, so was the kissing of the tips of the gloves to the horsemen who cantered by. There was quite a kingly dignity full of benevolence in the nods bestowed here and there upon fishers and boatmen in dingy flannel trousers rising to the arm-pits, trousers that looked as if they would have stood alone. Then there was an encounter with a brace of beaux, a halt, the raising and replacing of their hats, and the snuff-box of the Master of the Ceremonies flashed in the bright autumn sunshine as it was offered to each in turn, and pinches were taken of the highly-scented Prince's Mixture out of the historical prince's present—a solid golden, deeply-chased, and massive box. Then there was a loud snuffling noise; three expirations of three breaths in a loud 'Hah!' three snappings of three fingers and three thumbs, the with-drawal of three bandanna silk, gold, and scarlet handker-chiefs, to flip away a little snuff from three shirt frills; then the snuff-box flashed and glistened as it was held behind the Master of the Ceremonies, with his gold-mounted whip; three hats were raised again and replaced, their wearers having mutually decided that the day was charming, and Sir Harry Payne, officer of dragoons in mufti, like his chosen companion, Sir Matthew Bray, went one way to 'ogle the gyurls,' the Master of Ceremonies the other to reach the pier.

Everyone knew him; everyone sought and returned his bow. Fashion's high priest, the ruler of the destinies of many in the season, he was not the man to slight, and the gatekeeper drew back, hat in hand, and the bandmaster bowed low, as with pointed toes, graceful carriage, snuff-box in one hand, eye-glass and whip for the horse he never rode in the other, Stuart Denville walked behind the mask he wore, mincing, and bowing, and condescending, past the groups that dotted the breezy resort.

Half-way down the pier, but almost always hat in hand, and the set smile deepening the lines about his well-cut mouth, he became aware of some excitement towards the end.

There was a shriek and then a babble of voices talking, cries for a boat, and a rush to the side, where a lady, who had arrived in a bath-chair, pushed by a tall footman in mourning livery, surmounted by a huge braided half-moon hat, was gesticulating wildly and going to and fro, now fanning herself with a monstrous black fan, now closing it with a snap, and tapping lady bystanders with it on the shoulder or arm.

'He'll be drowned. I'm sure he'll be drowned. Why is there no boatman? Why is there no help? Oh, here is dear Mr. Denville. Oh! Mr. Denville, help, help, help!'

Here the lady half turned round, and made with each cry of 'help!' a backward step towards the Master of the Ceremonies, who had not accelerated his pace a whit, for fear of losing grace, and who was only just in time—the lady managed that—to catch her as she half leaned against his arm.

'Dear Lady Drelincourt, what terrible accident has befallen us here?'

'My darling!' murmured the lady. 'Save him, oh, save him, or I shall die!'

CHAPTER X.

A SMALL RESCUE.

SMALL matters make great excitements among idle seaside people, and as Denville gracefully helped Lady Drelincourt to a chair, and stepped mincingly to the side of the pier, he found that the little crowd were gazing down upon the black, snub-nosed, immature bull-dog physiognomy of an extremely fat Chinese pug dog, who, in a fit of playfulness with another fashionable dog, had forgotten his proximity to the extreme edge of the pier and gone in with a splash.

He had swum round and round, evidently mistrustful of his powers to reach the shore, and, in a very stolid manner, appeared to enjoy his bath; but growing tired, he had ceased to swim, and, throwing up his glistening black muzzle, had begun to beat the water with his forepaws, uttering from time to time a dismal yelp, while a bell attached to his collar gave a ting. Ignorant of the fact that he was fat enough to float if he only kept still, he was fast approaching the state when chicken legs and macaroons

would tempt in vain, when his stiffened jaws would refuse
to ope to the tiny ratafia well soaked in milk, and digestion
pains would assail him no more, after too liberal an in-
dulgence in the well-fried cutlet of juicy veal. The bell-
hung pagoda in Lady Drelincourt's drawing-room was likely
to be vacant till another pet was bought, and as the Master
of the Ceremonies gazed down at poor Titi through his glass,
it was in time to see a rough fisherman throw a rope in
rings to the drowning beast, evidently under the impression
that the dog would seize the rope and hold on till he was
drawn up, for no boat was near.

The rope was well aimed, for it struck the pet heavily,
knocking him under, and the rough boatman took off
his glazed hat, and scratched a very rough head, staring in wonderment at the effect of his well-meant
effort.

But Titi came up again and yelped loudly, this time with
a sweet, silvery, watery gurgle in his throat.

Then he turned over, and a lady shrieked. Then he
paddled about on his side, and made a foam in the water,
and in spite of the helpless, sympathising glances given
through the gold-rimmed eyeglass of the Master of the
Ceremonies, Titi must have been drowned had there not
been a sudden splash from the staging of the pier somewhere below, a loud exciting cry, and a figure seen to rise
from its plunge, swim steadily to the drowning dog, reach it

amidst a storm of delighted cries, swim back to the staging, and disappear.

This was the correct time, and Lady Drelincourt fainted dead away, with her head resting upon her shoulder, and her shoulder on the back of her chair. Immediately there was a rustling in bow-decked reticules, smelling salts were drawn, and Lady Drelincourt's nose was attacked. She was almost encircled with cut-glass bottles.

The Master of the Ceremonies looked on, posed in an attitude full of eager interest, and he saw, what was nothing new to his attentive gaze, that Time had behaved rudely to Lady Drelincourt; that art had been called in to hide his ravages, and that her ladyship's attitude caused cracks in the thickened powder, and that it differed in tone from the skin beneath; that there was a boniness of bust, and an angularity of shoulder where it should have been round and soft; and that if her ladyship fainted much more he would not be answerable for the consequences to her head of hair.

But Lady Drelincourt was not going to faint much more. The dog had been saved, and she had fanted enough, so that at the first approach of a rude hand to loosen the fastenings at her throat, she sighed and gasped, struggled faintly, opened her eyes of belladonna brilliancy, stared wildly round, recovered her senses, and exclaimed:

‘ Where is he ? Where is my Titi ? Where is his preserver ?’ and somebody said, ‘ Here !’

There was a hurried opening of the circle, and Stuart Denville, Esquire, Master of the Ceremonies, struck a fresh attitude full of astonishment, but, like the rest of the well-dressed throng, he shrank away, as a tall, fair youth, dripping with water, which made his hair and clothes cling closely, came from an opening that led to the piles below, squeezing the pug to free him from moisture, and gazing from face to face.

'You rascally prodigal!' whispered the Master of the Ceremonies, as the youth came abreast, 'you've been fishing for dabs again!'

'Well, suppose I have,' said the youth sulkily.

'Where is his preserver? Give me back my darling Titi,' wailed Lady Drelincourt; and catching the wet fat dog to her breast, regardless of the effect upon her rich black silk dress and crape, the little beast uttered a satisfied yelp and nestled up to her, making a fat jump upwards so as to lick a little of the red off the lady's lips.

'And who was it saved you, my precious?' sobbed the lady.

'Lady Drelincourt,' said the Master of the Ceremonies, taking the youth's hand gingerly, with one glove, 'allow me to introduce your dear pet's preserver—it was Morton Denville, Lady Drelincourt, my son. I am sorry he is so very wet.'

'Bless you—bless you!' cried Lady Drelincourt with

effusion. 'I could embrace you, you brave and gallant man, but—but—not now.'

'No, no—not now. Lady Drelincourt, let me assist you to your chair. Morton,' he whispered, 'you're like a scarecrow: quick, be off. You dog, if you mind me now, your fortune's made.'

'Oh, is it, father? Well, I'm precious glad. I say, isn't it cold?'

'Yes: quick—home, and change your things. Stop; where are you going?'

'Down below, to fetch the dabs.'

'D—— the dabs, sir,' whispered the Master of the Ceremonies excitedly; 'you'll spoil the effect. Run, sir, run!'

The youth hesitated a moment and then started and ran swiftly towards the cliff, amidst a shrill burst of cheers, the ladies fluttering their handkerchiefs, and fisherman Dick Miggles wishing he had been that there boy.

'Denville—dear Denville,' said her ladyship, 'how proud you must be of such a son!'

'The idol of my life, dear Lady Drelincourt,' said the Master of the Ceremonies, arranging her dress in the bath-chair. 'Shall I carry the poor dog?'

'No, no—no, no, my darling Titi!' cried the lady, to his great relief. 'Thomas, take me home quickly,' she said, as the wet dog nestled in her crape lap and uttered a few snuffles of satisfaction. 'Quick, or Titi will take cold Denville, see me safely home. My nerves are gone.'

'The shock, of course.'

'Yes, Denville, and I shall never forget your gallant son,' sobbed her ladyship hysterically, as they passed through a lane of promenaders; 'but I must not cry.'

It was indeed quite evident that such a giving way to natural feeling would have had serious results, and she was not veiled. So the rising tear was sent back, and Denville saw her safely home, forgetting for the moment his domestic troubles in his exultation, and making out a future for his son, as the rich Lady Drelincourt's protégé—a commission —a handsome allowance. Perhaps—ah, who knew! Such unions had taken place before now.

For the next half-hour he was living artificially, seeing his son advanced in life, and his daughter dwelling in a kind of fairy castle that had been raised through Lady Drelincourt's introduction.

Then as he approached home a black cloud seemed to come down and close him in, the artificiality was gone, age seemed to be attacking him, and he moaned as he reached the door.

'Heaven help me, and give me strength to keep up this actor's life, for I'm very, very weak.'

CHAPTER XI.

THE OPENING OF A VEIN.

'WELL, young Denville,' said Dick Miggles, the great swarthy fisherman, whose black hair, dark eyes, and aquiline features told that his name was a corruption of Miguel, and that he was a descendant of one of the unfortunates who had been wrecked and imprisoned when the Spanish Armada came to grief, and had finally resolved to 'remain an Englishman.'

Dick Miggles rarely did anything in the daytime but doze and smoke. Of course, he ate and drank, and, as on the present occasion, nursed the little girl that Mrs. Miggles, who was as round and snub and English of aspect as her lord was Spanish, had placed in his arms. At night matters were different, and people did say——but never mind.

'Well, young Denville,' said Fisherman Dick, as he sat on the bench outside his whitewashed cottage with the whelk-shell path, bordered with marigold beds, one of which flowers he picked from time to time to give the child.

'Well, Dick, where are my dabs?'

'Haw-haw,' said the fisherman, laughing. 'I say, missus, where's them dabs?'

Mrs. Miggles was washing up the dinner things, and she came out with a dish on which were a number of fried heads and tails, with a variety of spinal and other bones.

'What a shame!' cried Morton, with a look of disgust. 'I do call that shabby, Dick.'

'How was I to know that you would come after 'em, lad? I'd ha' brote 'em, but I don't like to come to your house now.'

'I say, Dick, don't be a fool,' cried the lad. 'What's the good of raking up that horrid affair, now it's all dead and buried?'

'Nay,' said Dick, shaking his head. 'That ar'n't all dead and buried, like the old woman, my lad. There's more trouble to come out o' that business yet.'

'Oh, stuff and nonsense!'

'Nay, it isn't, my lad. Anyhow, I don't like coming to your place now, and there's other reasons as well, ar'n't there, missus?'

'Now, I do call that shabby, Dick. Just because there's a bill owing for fish. I've told you I'll pay it some day, if papa does not; I mean, when I have some money.'

'Ay, so you did, lad, and so you will, I know; but I didn't mean that, did I, missus?'

'No,' came from within.

'What did you mean, then?'

'Never mind. You wait and see. I say, the old gentleman looks as if he'd got over the trouble, Master Morton. He was quite spry to-day.'

'No, he hasn't,' said Morton. 'It's quite horrible at home. He's ill, and never hardly speaks, and my sister frets all day long.'

'Do she though! Poor gal! Ah, she wants it found out, my lad. It wherrits her, because you see it's just as if them jools of the old lady's hung like to your folk, and you'd got to account for 'em.'

'Get out! Why, what nonsense, Dick.'

'What, dropped it agen, my pretty?' said the great fisherman, stooping to pick up a flower, and place it in the little fat hand that was playing with his big rough finger. 'Ah, well, perhaps it be, but never mind. I say, though, the old gentleman looked quite hisself agen. My! he do go dandy-jacking along the cliff, more'n the best of 'em. He do make me laugh, he do. Why, hello, Master Morton, lad, what's matter?'

'If you dare to laugh at my father, Dick,' cried the boy, whose face was flushed and eyes flashing, 'big as you are, I'll punch your head.'

'Naw, naw, naw, don't do that, my lad,' said the fisherman, growing solemn directly. 'I were not laughing at him. I were laughing at his clothes.'

' And if my father dresses like the Prince and the Duke and all the fashionable gentlemen, what is there to laugh at then ?   Suppose I were to laugh at you for living in that great pair of trousers that come right up under your arms ?'

' Well, you might, lad, and welcome ; they're very comf'table.   P'r'aps you'd like to laugh at my boots.   Haw, haw, haw, Master Morton, what d'yer think I did yes'day ? I took little flower here, after missus had washed her, and put her right into one o' my boots, and she stood up in it with her head and arms out, laughing and crowing a good 'un.   Ar'n't she a little beauty ?'

' Yes,' said Morton, looking down and playing with the child.   ' Whose is she ?'

' Dunno.   Ask the missus.'

' And she won't tell me, Dick.'

' That's so.   But look here, lad.   I'm sorry I laughed at Master Denville, for he's a nice gentleman, and always has a kind word and a smile, if he doesn't pay his bill.'

' Dick !'

' All right, my lad, all right.   You'll pay that when you're rich.   I say : chaps sez as you'll marry Lady Drelincourt, now, after saving her dog, and——'

' Don't be a fool, Dick.   Here, what were you going to say ?' said the lad, reddening.

' You won't want a bit of fishing then, I suppose ?'

'Look here; are you going to speak, Dick, or am I to go?'

'All right, my lad. Look here; we eat your dabs, but never mind them. I shall just quietly leave a basket at your door to-night. You needn't know anything about it, and you needn't be too proud to take it, for a drop in the house is worth a deal sometimes, case o' sickness. It's real French sperit, and a drop would warm the old gentleman sometimes when he is cold.'

'Smuggling again, Dick?'

'Never you mind about that, Master Morton, and don't call things by ugly names. But that ar'n't all I've got to say. You lost your dabs, but if you'll slip out to-night and come down the pier, the tide'll be just right, and I'll have the bait and lines ready, and I'll give you as good a bit of fishing as you'd wish to have.'

'Will you, Dick?'

'Ay, that I will. They were on last night, but they'll be wonderful to-night, and I shouldn't wonder if we ketches more than we expex.'

'Oh, but I couldn't go, Dick.'

'Why not, lad?'

'You see, I should have to slip out in the old way— through the drawing-room, and down the balcony pillar.'

'Same as you and Master Fred used, eh?'

'Don't talk about him,' said the lad.

'Well, he's your own brother.'

'Yes, but father won't have his name mentioned,' said the boy sadly. 'He's to be dead to us. Here, what a fool I am, talking so to you!'

'Oh, I don't know, my lad; we was always friends, since you was quite a little chap, and I used to give you rides in my boat.'

'Yes; you always were a friend, Dick, and I like you.'

'On'y you do get a bit prouder now you're growing such a strapping chap, Master Morton.'

'I shan't change to you, Dick.'

'Then come down to-night, say at half arter 'leven.'

Morton shook his head.

'Why, you ar'n't afraid o' seeing the old woman's ghost, are you?'

'Absurd! No. But it seems so horrible to come down that balcony pillar to get out on the sly.'

'Why, you never used to think so, my lad.'

'No, but I do now. Do you know, Dick,' he said in a whisper, 'I often think that the old lady was killed by some one who had watched me go in and out that way.'

'Eh?' cried the fisherman, giving a peculiar stare.

'Yes, I do,' said the lad, laying his hand on the big fellow's shoulders. 'I feel sure of it, for that murder must have been done by some one who knew how easy it was to get up there and open the window.'

'Did you ever see anyone watching of you?' said the fisherman in a hoarse whisper.

'N—no, I'm not sure. I fancy I did see some one watching one night.'

'Phew!' whistled the fisherman; 'it's rather hot, my lad, sitting here in the sun.'

'Perhaps some day I shall find out who did it, Dick.'

'Hah—yes,' said the man, staring at him hard. 'Then you won't come?'

'Yes, I will,' cried Morton. 'It's so cowardly not to come. I shall be there;' and, stopping to pick up the flower the child had again dropped, the pretty little thing smiled in his face, and he bent down and kissed it before striding away.

'Think o' that, now,' said Mrs. Miggles, coming to the door.

'Think o' what?' growled her lord, breaking off an old sea-ditty he was singing to the child.

'Why, him taking to the little one and kissing it. How strange things is!'

CHAPTER XII.

'Gad, but the old boy's proud of that chariot,' said Sir
Matthew Bray, mystifying his sight by using an eyeglass.

'Yes,' said Sir Harry Payne, who was lolling against the
railings that guarded promenaders from a fall over the cliff;
and he joined his friend in gazing at an elegantly-appointed
britzka which had drawn up at the side, and at whose door
the Master of the Ceremonies was talking to a very young
and pretty woman. 'Yes; deuced pretty woman, May
Burnett. What a shame that little wretch Frank should
get hold of her.'

'Egad, but it was a good thing for her. I say, Harry,
weren't you sweet upon her?'

'I never tell tales out of school, Matt. 'Fore George, how
confoundedly my head aches this morning.'

Just then the Master of the Ceremonies drew back, raising
his hat with the greatest of politeness to the lady, and waving

his cane to the coachman, who drove off, the old man going in the other direction muttering to himself, but proud and happy, while the carriage passed the two bucks, who raised their hats and were rewarded with the sweetest of smiles from a pair of very innocent, girlish-looking little lips, their owner, aptly named May, being a very blossom of girlish prettiness and dimpled innocency.

'Gad, she is pretty,' said Sir Matthew Bray. 'Come along, old lad. Let's see if Drelincourt or anyone else is on the pier.'

'Aha! does the wind blow that way, Matt? Why were you not there to save the dog?'

'Wind? what way?' said the big, over-dressed dandy, raising his eyebrows.

'Ha—ha—ha! come, come!' cried Sir Harry, touching his friend in the side with the gold knob of his cane, 'how innocent we are;' and, taking Sir Matthew's arm, they strolled on towards the pier.

'I didn't ask you who the note was for that we left at Mother Clode's,' said Sir Matthew sulkily.

'No; neither did I ask you where yours came from—you Goliath of foxes,' laughed Sir Harry. 'But I say. 'Fore George, it was on mourning paper, and was scented with musk. Ha—ha—ha!'

Sir Matthew scowled and grumbled, but the next moment the incident was forgotten, and both gentlemen were raising their ugly beaver hats to first one and then another of the belles they passed.

Meanwhile the britzka was driven on along the Parade, and drew up at the house of the Master of the Ceremonies, where the footman descended from his seat beside the coachman, and brought envious lodging-letters to the windows on either side by his tremendous roll of the knocker and peal at the bell.

Isaac appeared directly.

Yes, Miss Denville was in, so the steps were rattled down, and Mrs. Frank Burnett descended lightly, rustled up to the front door, and entered with all the hauteur of one accustomed to a large income and carriage calling.

' Ah, Claire darling!' she cried, as she was shown into the drawing-room; ' how glad I shall be to see you doing this sort of thing.   Really, you know, it is time.'

' Ah, May dear,' said Claire, kissing her sister affectionately, but with a grave pained look in her eyes, ' I am so glad to see you.   I was wishing you would come.   Papa will be so disappointed: he has gone up the town to see the tailor about Morton.'

' What, does that boy want new clothes again? Papa did not say so.'

' Have you seen him, then ?'

' Yes.   How well he looks.   But why did you want to see me ?'

For answer Claire took her sister's hand, led her to the chintz-covered sofa, and seated herself beside her, with her arm round May's waist.

'Oh, do be careful, Claire,' said Mrs. Burnett pettishly ; 'this is my lute-string. And, my dear, how wretchedly you do dress in a morning.'

'It is good enough for home, dear, and we are obliged to be so careful. May dear, I hardly like to ask you, but could you spare me a guinea or two?'

'Spare you a guinea or two? Why, bless the child! what can you want with a guinea or two?'

'I want it for Morton. There are several things he needs so much, and I want besides to be able to let him have a little pocket-money when he asks.'

'Oh, really, I cannot, Claire. It is quite out of the question. Frank keeps me so dreadfully short. You would never believe what trouble I have to get a few guineas from him when I am going out, and there is so much play now that one is compelled to have a little to lose. But I must be off. I have some shopping to do, and a call or two to make besides. Then there is a book to get at Miss Clode's. I won't ask you to come for a drive this morning.

'No, dear, don't. But stay a few minutes ; I have something to say to you.'

'Now, whatever can you have to say, Claire dear? Nothing about that—that—oh, don't, pray. I could not bear it. All the resolution I had was needed to come here at all, and, as I told you in my letter, it was impossible for me to come before. Frank would not let me.'

' I want to talk to you very—very seriously.'

' About that dreadful affair?'

' No,' said Claire, with a curiously solemn look coming over her face, and her voice assuming a deep, tragic tone.

' Then it is about—oh, Claire !' she cried passionately, as she glanced up at a floridly painted portrait of herself on the wall; ' I do wish you would take that picture down.'

' Why should you mind that ? You know papa likes it.'

' Because it reminds me so of the past.'

' When you were so weak and frivolous with that poor fellow Louis.'

' Now I did not come here to be scolded,' cried the child-like little thing passionately. ' I don't care. I did love poor Louis, and he'd no business to go away and die.'

' Hush, hush, May, my darling,' said Claire, with a pained face. ' I did not scold you.'

' You did,' sobbed the other; ' you said something about Louis, and that you had something to talk to me about. What is it ?' she cried with a look of childish fright in her eyes. ' What is it ?' she repeated, and she clung to her sister excitedly.

' Hush, hush, May, I was not going to scold, only to talk to you.'

'It will keep, I'm sure,' cried May, with the scared look intensifying.

'No, dearest, it will not keep, for it is something very serious—so serious that I would not have our father know it for the world.'

'Lack-a-day, Claire,' cried Mrs. Burnett, with assumed mirth forming pleasant dimples in her sweet childish face, 'what is the matter?'

'I wanted to say a few words of warning to you, May dear. You know how ready people are to gossip?'

'Good lack, yes, indeed they are. But what——?' she faltered, 'what——?'

'And several times lately they have been busy with your name.'

'With my name!' cried Mrs. Burnett, with a forced laugh, and a sigh of relief.

'Yes, dear, about little bits of freedom, and—and—I don't like to call it coquetry. I want you, dearest, to promise me that you will be a little more staid. Dear May, it pains me more than I can say.'

'Frump! frump! frump! Why you silly, weak, quakerish old frump, Claire! What nonsense to be sure! A woman in my position, asked out as I am to rout, and kettledrum, and ball, night after night, cannot sit mumchance against the wall, and mumble scandal with the old maids. Now, I wonder who has been putting all this in your head?'

' I will not repeat names, dear; but it is some one whom I can trust.'

' Then she is a scandalous old harridan, whoever she is,' cried Mrs. Burnett with great warmth. ' And what do you know about such matters?'

' I know it pains me to hear that my dear sister's name is mentioned freely at the officers' mess, and made a common toast.'

' Oh, indeed, madam ; and pray what about yours ? Who is talked of at every gathering, and married to everyone in turn ?'

' I know nothing of those things,' said Claire coldly.

' Ah, well, all right; but, I say, when's it to be, Claire ? Don't fribble away this season. I hear of two good opportunities for you ; and—oh, I say, Claire, they do tell me that a certain gentleman said—a certain very high personage—that you were——'

' Shame, sister !' cried Claire, starting up as if she had been stung. ' How can you—how dare you, speak to me like that ?'

' Hoity-toity ! What's the matter, child ?'

' Child !' cried Claire indignantly. ' Do you forget that you have always been as a child to me—my chief care ever since our mother died ? Oh, May, May, darling, this is not like you. Pray—pray be more guarded in what you say. There, dearest, I am not angry ; but this light and frivolous manner distresses me. You are Frank Burnett's honoured wife—girl yet, I know ; but your marriage lifts you at once to a position amongst women, and these light, flippant ways sit so ill upon one like you.'

'Oh, pooh ! stuff ! you silly, particular old frump !' cried May sharply. 'Do you suppose that a married woman is going to be like a weak, prudish girl ? There, there, there ; I did not come to quarrel, and I won't be scolded. I say, they tell me that handsome Major Rockley is likely to throw himself away on Cora Dean.'

'Oh, May, May, my darling !'

'You are a goose not to catch him in your own net.'

'Major Rockley ?'

'Yes ; he is rich and handsome. I wish I'd had him instead of Frank.'

'May, dear May !'

'Oh, I know : it's only talk. But, I say, dear, have you heard about old Drelincourt ? So shocking ! In mourning, too. They say she is mad to marry some one. There, good-bye. Don't crush my bonnet. Oh, of course ; yes, I'm going to be as prudish as you, and so careful. Well, what is it ?'

'May, you cannot deceive me ; you have something on your mind.'

'I ? Nonsense ! Absurd !'

'You were going to tell me something ; to ask me to help you, I am sure.'

'Well—perhaps—yes,' said the little thing, with scarlet face. 'But you frightened me out of it. I daren't now. Next time. Good-bye ; good-bye ; good-bye.'

She rattled these last words out hastily, kissed her sister, and hurried, in a strangely excited manner, from the room.

Claire watched the carriage go, and then sank back out of sight in a chair, to clasp her hands upon her knees, and gaze before her with a strangely old look upon her beautiful face.

For there was trouble, not help, to be obtained from the wilful, girlish wife who had so lately left her side.

CHAPTER XIII.

A NIGHT-BIRD TRAPPED.

It was, as Morton Denville said, cold and cheerless at his home, and the proceedings that night endorsed his words, as at half-past ten, after the servants had been dismissed, his father rose to seek his sleepless couch.

Claire rose at the same moment, starting from a silent musing fit, while Morton threw down the book he had been reading in a very ill-used way.

'Good-night, my son,' said Denville, holding out his hand, and grasping the lad's with unusual fervour.

'Good-night, father.'

'And you'll mind and be particular now, my boy. I am sure that at last I can advance your prospects.'

'Oh, yes, father, I'll be particular.'

'Don't let people see you fishing there again.'

'No, father, I'll take care. Good-night. Coming Claire?'

Claire had put away her needlework, and was standing cold and silent by the table.

'Good-night, Claire, my child,' said Denville, with a piteous look and appeal in his tone.

'Good-night, father.'

She did not move as the old man took a couple of steps forward and kissed her brow, laying his hands afterwards upon her head and muttering a blessing.

Then, in spite of her efforts, a chill seemed to run through her, and she trembled, while he, noting it, turned away with a look of agony in his countenance that he sought to conceal, and sank down in the nearest chair.

He seemed to be a totally different man, and those who had seen him upon the cliff and pier would not have recognised in him the fashionable fribble, whose task it was to direct the flight of the butterflies of the Assembly Room, and preside at every public dance.

'Aren't you going to bed, father?' said Morton, trying to speak carelessly.

'Yes, yes, my son, yes. I only wish to think out my plans a little—your commission, and other matters.'

'I hope he won't be long,' muttered Morton as he left the room. 'Why, Claire, how white and cold you are! There, hang me if it isn't enough to make a fellow sell himself to that old Lady Drelincourt for the sake of getting money to take care of you. If I'd got plenty, you should go abroad for a change.'

Claire kissed him affectionately.

'Hang me if I don't begin to hate May. She doesn't seem like a sister to us. Been here to-day, hasn't she? I heard they'd come back.'

'Yes,' said Claire with a sigh.

'It was cowardly of them to go off like that, when you were in such trouble. You did not have a single woman come and say a kind word when —— *that* was in the house.'

'Don't speak of it, dear,' said Claire. 'Mrs. Barclay came, though.'

'Rum old girl! I always feel ready to laugh at her.'

'She has a heart of gold.'

'Old Barclay has a box of gold, and nice and tightly he keeps it locked up. I say, he'll sell us up some day.'

'Morton dear, I can't bear to talk to you to-night; and don't speak like that of May. She has her husband to obey.'

'Bless him!' cried Morton musingly. 'Good-night, Sis.'

He kissed her affectionately, and a faint smile came into Claire's wan face, as it seemed to comfort her in her weary sorrow. Then they parted, and she went to her room, opened the window, and sat with her face among the flowers, watching the sea and thinking of some one whom she had in secret seen pass by there at night.

That was a dream of the past, she told herself now, for it could never be. Love, for her, was dead; no man could call her wife with such a secret as she held in her breast, and as she thought on, her misery seemed greater than she could bear.

The tide was well up, and the stars glittered in the heaving bosom of the sea as she sat and gazed out; and then all at once her heart seemed to stand still, and then began beating furiously, for a familiar step came slowly along the cobble-paved walk in front of the house, along by the railed edge of the cliff, and then for a moment she could see the tall, dark figure she knew so well, gazing wistfully up at the window.

She knew he loved her; she knew that her heart had gone out to him, though their acquaintance was of the most distant kind. She knew, too, how many obstacles poverty had thrown in the way of both, but some day, she had felt, all would be swept away. Now all that was past. She must never look at him again.

She shrank from the window, and sank upon her knees, weeping softly for the unattainable, as she felt how he must love her, and that his heart was with her in sympathy with all her trouble.

'Dead—dead—dead,' she moaned; 'my love is dead, and my life-course broadly marked out, so that I cannot turn to the right or left.'

She started and shuddered, for below her there was the tread of a heavy foot. She heard her father's slight cough, and his closing door, and at the same moment, as if it were he who separated them, the step outside could be heard returning, and Claire arose and crept to the window again to listen till it died away.

'Dead—dead—my love is dead,' she moaned again, and closing the window, she strove to forget her agony of mind and the leaden weight that seemed to rest upon her brow in sleep.

Eleven had struck, and two quarters had chimed before Morton Denville dared to stir. He had waited with open door, listening impatiently for his father's retiring; he had listened to the steps outside; and then at last, with all the eagerness of a boy, in spite of his near approach to manhood, and excited by the anticipations of the fishing, and the romance of the little adventure, he stole forth with his shoes in his hands, after carefully closing the catch of his well-oiled door.

The crucial part was the passing of the end of the passage leading to his father's room, and here he paused for a few moments, but he fancied he could hear a long-drawn breathing, and, after a hasty glance at the door of the back drawing-room, erst Lady Teigne's chamber, he opened the drawing-room door, stepped in and closed it.

He breathed more freely now, but a curious chill ran

through him, and he felt ready to retreat as he saw that the folding doors were not closed, and that the faint light from the back window made several articles of furniture look grotesque and strange.

'Here am I, just twenty, and as cowardly as a girl,' he muttered. 'I won't be afraid.'

All the same, though, his heart beat violently, and he shrank from moving for some minutes.

'And Dick waiting,' he muttered.

Those words gave him the strength he sought, and, going on tiptoe across the room, half feeling as if a hand were going to be laid upon his shoulder to keep him back, he drew aside the blind, opened the French window, passed out, closed it after him, and stood there in the balcony, gazing at the heaving, star-spangled sea.

'I can't be a man yet,' he said to himself. 'If I were I shouldn't feel so nervous. It is very horrid, though, the first time after that old woman was killed; and by some one coming up there. Ugh! it's very creepy. I half fancied I could hear the old girl snoring as she used.'

He leaned over the balcony rails and looked to right and left, but all seemed silent in the sleeping town, and after listening for a minute or two he seized the support of the balcony roof, stepped over the rails, lowered himself a little, and clasping the pillar with his legs, slid easily down, rested for a moment on the railings with his feet between the spikes, and then, clasping the pillar, dropped lightly down upon the pavement, to be seized by two strong hands by arm and throat, a dark figure having stepped out of the doorway to hold him fast.

CHAPTER XIV.

SOMETHING THROWN IN THE SEA.

'What——'

'Hush! Who are you? What are you doing here? Why, Morton Denville!'

'Richard Linnell! Is it you? Oh, I say, you did give me a scare. I thought it was that chap come again.'

'What do you mean?'

'Why, the fellow who did that, you know,' said the lad with a nod upwards.

'But why have you stolen down like this, sir?'

'Don't talk so loud; you'll wake the old man. Only going fishing.'

'Fishing? Now?'

'Yes. Fisherman Dick's waiting for me on the pier.'

'Is this true?' asked Linnell sternly.

'True! What do you mean?' said the lad haughtily. 'Did you ever know a Denville tell a lie?'

'No, of course not. But it looks bad, young fellow, to

see you stealing out of the house like this, and after that ghastly affair.'

'Hush, don't talk about it,' said the lad with a shudder. 'But, I say, how came you here?'

'I—I——' stammered Linnell. 'Oh, I was walking along the cliff and I saw the window open. I thought something was wrong, and I crossed to see.'

'Did you think some one had come to run away with my sister, Mr. Linnell?' said the lad with a sneering laugh. 'Ah, well, you needn't have been alarmed, and if they had it would have been no business of yours.'

Richard Linnell drew his breath with a faint hiss.

'That's rather a sneering remark, young gentleman,' he said coldly; 'but there, I don't want to quarrel with you.'

'All the same to me if you did, only if you will take a bit of good advice, stop at home, and don't be hanging about gentlemen's houses at this time of night. It looks bad. There, now you can knock at the door and ring them up and tell them I've gone fishing. I don't care.'

He thrust his hands in his pockets and strutted away, trying to appear very manly and independent, but nature would not permit him to look like anything but a big, overgrown boy.

Richard Linnell drew his breath again with the same low hiss, and stood watching the retiring figure, after which he followed the boy along the cliff till he saw him reach the pier, where a gruff voice greeted him ; and, satisfied that the truth had been spoken, he turned off and went home.

'Thought you wasn't coming, lad,' said Fisherman Dick. 'Here, just you ketch hold o' yon basket, and let's get to work.'

Morton seized the basket of bait, and together they walked to the very end of the pier, at one corner of which was a gangway and some steps, down which they went to a platform of open beams, moist with spray, and only about a foot above the water now the tide was high, the promenade forming the ceiling above their heads.

It was very dark, and the damp, salt smell of the weed that hung to the piles was floating around, while the misty spray every now and then moistened their hands and faces. On all sides huge square wooden piles rose up, looking grim and strange in the gloom, and before them the star-spangled sea heaved and sank, and heaved and sighed and whispered in amongst the woodwork, every now and then seeming to give a hungry smack as if the waves were the lips of some monstrous mouth, trying to seize upon the two fishers for its prey.

'Didn't I tell you ?' said Dick Miggles : 'Sea's just right, and the fish'll bite like anything. We ought to get ten shillings' worth to-night. There you are ; go ahead.'

Dick had been busy unwinding a line, whose hooks he had already baited ; and then, for the next quarter of an hour they were busy catching and hauling in whiting and large dabs, and every now and then a small conger, the basket filling rapidly.

Then, all at once, the fish ceased biting, and they sat waiting and feeling the lines, trying to detect a touch.

' Some one coming,' said Dick suddenly, in a low whisper. ' What's he want to-night ?'

' Sh !' whispered back Morton. ' Don't speak, or I shall be found out.'

' Right,' answered Dick in the same low tone ; and as they sat there in the darkness with the water lapping just beneath them, and a wave coming in among the piles every now and then with a hiss and a splash, they could hear the slow, firm tread of some one coming down the pier, right to the end, to stand there as if listening, quite still above their heads.

All at once the night-breeze wafted to them the scent of a good cigar, and they knew that whoever it was must be smoking.

At the same moment, Morton felt a tug at his line, and he knew a fish had hooked itself.

It was all he could do to keep from dragging it in ; but he was, in spite of his boasting, afraid of his nocturnal expedition coming to his father's ears, and he remained still.

Fisherman Dick had moved so silently that Morton had not heard him ; but all at once the planks overhead seemed veined with light, and the figure of the fisherman could be seen dimly, with his face close up to a hole in the planking. The light died out as quickly as it shone, and the odour of tobacco diffused itself again, while the man overhead began to walk slowly up and down.

Tug-tug-tug! How that fish—a big one, too—did pull! But Morton resisted the temptation, and waited, till all at once it seemed to him that the smoker must have heard them, and was about to come down, for he was evidently listening.

Then there was a shuffling of feet, a curious expiration of the breath, and a sort of grunt, followed by utter silence; and then, some fifty yards away, right in front of where Morton sat, there was a faint golden splash in the sea, and the noise of, as it were, a falling stone or piece of wood.

Almost at the same moment Morton noticed that his line had become phosphorescent, and he could see it for some distance down as the fish he had hooked dragged it here and there.

Then there was a sigh overhead as of relief, and the steps were heard again, gradually going back along the pier, and dying slowly away.

Simultaneously, Morton Denville and the fisherman began hauling in their lines, the former listening the while, to make sure that the promenader did not return; and then, as all was silent, their captives were drawn on to the open plank-

ing, to break the silence with flapping and beating and
tangling the lines.

'What light was that, Dick?' said Morton, as he threw
his fish into the basket.

'Dunno, zackly. Some way o' lighting another cigar.'

'Who was it—could you see?'

'How's it likely I could see, squintin' through a hole like
that? Some 'un or 'nother stretching his legs, 'cause he
ain't got no work to do, I s'pose.'

'But couldn't you see his face?'

'See his face? Is it likely? Just you get up and look
through that hole. Why, I had to look straight up, then
sidewise, and then straight up again, and that bends your
sight about so as you couldn't even do anything with a spy-
glass.'

'I believe you could see who it was, and won't tell me.'

'Hear that, now! Why shouldn't I want to tell? Says
you, I'm out on the sly, and nobody mustn't know I'm
here.'

'No, I didn't,' said Morton shortly.

'Well, lad, not in words you didn't; but that's how it
seemed to be, so I kep' as quiet as I could, and whoever it
was didn't hear us.'

'What did he throw into the water?'

'Stone, I s'pose. Some o' them dandy jacks, as looks as
if they couldn't move in their clothes, once they gets alone,

nothing they likes better than throwing stones in the water. If it wasn't that the waves washes 'em up again, they'd have throwed all Saltinville into the sea years ago.'

Two hours later, after a very successful night's sport, Morton parted from Fisherman Dick at the shore end of the pier, and ran home, while the owner of the lines and the heavy basket sat down on the lid, and rubbed the back of his head.

' Yes, I did see his face, as plain as I ever see one, but I warn't going to tell you so, Master Morton, my lad. What did he chuck inter the sea, and what did he chuck it there for ?'

Fisherman Dick sat thinking for a few minutes, and shaking his head, before saying aloud :

' No ; it didn't sound like a stone.'

After which he had another think, and then he got up, shouldered his basket, and went homeward, saying :

' I shall have to find out what that there was.'

CHAPTER XV.

MISS CLODE's library and fancy bazaar stood facing the sea—so near, indeed, that on stormy days she was occasionally compelled to have the green shutters up to protect the window-panes from the spray and shingle that were driven across the road. But on fine days it was open to the sunshine, and plenty of cane-seated chairs were ranged about the roomy shop.

The back was formed of a glass partition, pretty well covered with books, but not so closely as to hide the whole shop from the occupants of the snug parlour, where little, thin Miss Clode sat one fine morning, like a dried specimen of her niece, Annie Slade, a stout young lady nicknamed Dumpling by the bucks who made the place a sort of social exchange.

The shop was well fitted and carpeted. Glass cases, filled with gaily-dyed wools and silks, were on the counter. Glass cases were behind filled with knick-knacks and fancy goods, papier-maché trays and inkstands bright with mother-of-pearl, and ivory and ebony specimens of the turner's art. Look where you would, everything was brightly polished, and every speck of dust had been duly hunted out. In fact, Miss Clode's establishment whispered of prosperity, and suggested that the little eager-eyed maiden lady must be in the circumstances known as comfortable.

Business had not been very brisk that morning, but several customers had called to make purchases or to change books, and two of these latter had made purchases as well. In fact, it was rather curious, but when certain of her clients called, and Miss Clode introduced to their notice some special novelty, they always bought it without further consideration.

'You are such a clever business woman, auntie,' drawled her niece. 'I wish I could sell things as fast as you.'

'Perhaps you will some day, my dear.'

'Lady Drelincourt bought that little Tunbridge needle-book for half a guinea, didn't she, aunt?'

'Yes, my dear,' said Miss Clode, pursing up her thin lips.

'She couldn't have wanted it, auntie,' drawled the girl. 'I don't believe she ever used a needle in her life.'

'Perhaps not, my dear, but she might want it for a present.'

'Oh, so she might; I never thought of that. Customers!' added the girl sharply, and rose to go into the shop.

'I'll attend to them, my dear,' said Miss Clode quickly, and she entered the shop to smilingly confront Sir Harry Payne and Sir Matthew Bray.

'Well, Miss Clode, what's the newest and best book for a man to read?'

'Really, Sir Harry, I am very sorry,' she said. 'The coach has not brought anything fresh, but I expect a parcel down some time to-day. Perhaps you'd look in again?'

'Ah, well, I will,' he said. 'Come along, Bray.'

'Have you seen these new card-cases, Sir Matthew?' said the little woman, taking half a dozen from a drawer. 'They are real russia, and the gilding is of very novel design. Only a guinea, Sir Matthew, and quite new.'

'Ah, yes, very handsome indeed. A guinea, did you say?' he said, turning the handsome leather case over and over.

'Yes, Sir Matthew. May I put it down to your account?'

'Well, ah, yes—I—ah, yes, I'll take this one.'

'Thank you, Sir Matthew. I'll wrap it up, please, in silver paper;' and, with deft fingers, the little woman wrapped up the purchase, handed it over with a smile, and the two friends strolled out for Sir Harry to give his friend a light touch in the side with the head of his cane, accompanied by a peculiar smile, which the other refused to see.

'How very anxious Sir Harry seems to be to get that new book, auntie,' drawled Annie, coming into the shop where

Miss Clode was busily making an entry on her slate; 'that makes twice he's been here to-day.'

'Yes, my dear, he's a great reader. But now, Annie, the time has come when I think I may take you into my confidence.'

'La, auntie, do you?'

'I do, and mind this, child: if ever you are foolish or weak, or do anything to betray it, you leave me directly, and that will be a very serious thing.'

Miss Slade's jaw fell, and her mouth opened widely, as did her eyes.

'Ah, I see you understand, so now come here with me.'

Miss Slade obeyed, and followed her aunt into the middle room at the back, where, by means of a match dipped into a bottle of phosphorus. Miss Clode obtained a light and ignited a little roll of wax taper, and then, as her niece watched her with open eyes as they sat at the table, the lady took a small letter from her pocket and laid it with its sealed side uppermost on the table.

'Why, I saw Sir Harry Payne give you that letter this morning, auntie, when he came first.'

'Oh, you saw that, did you?' said Miss Clode.

'Yes, auntie, and I thought first he had given it to you to post, and then as you didn't send me with it, I wondered why he had written to you.'

'He did give it to me to post, my dear,' said Miss Clode

with a curious smile, 'and before I post it I am bound to see that he has not written anything that is not good for the la——person it is for.'

'Oh, yes, auntie, I see,' said Miss Slade, resting her fat cheeks on her fat fingers, and watching attentively as her aunt took out a seal from a tin box, one that looked as if it were made of putty, and compared it with the sealing-wax on the letter.

This being satisfactory, she cleverly held the wax to the little taper till it began to bubble and boil, when it parted easily, the paper being drawn open and only some silky threads of wax securing it, these being at once brushed aside.

'Oh, you have got it open lovely, auntie,' said the girl.

'Yes, my dear; and now I am going to read it,' said Miss Clode, suiting the deed to the word, skimming through the note rapidly, and then refolding it.

'Oh, I say, auntie, what does he say?' said the girl with her eyes sparkling.   'Is it about love?'

'Don't ask questions, and you will not get strange answers,' said Miss Clode austerely, as she deftly melted the wax once more, and applied the well-made bread seal, after which there was nothing to show that the letter had been opened.   'I see, though, that it was quite time I did trust you, my dear, and I hope I shall have no cause to repent.'

Just then a customer entered the shop, and again Miss Clode went to attend.

'I know it was a love-letter,' said Annie quickly; 'and it was Sir Harry Payne wrote it. I wonder who it was to. I wish he'd make love to me.'

Miss Clode came back directly with a volume of poems in her hand—a new copy, and looking significantly at her niece she said:

'I'm going to post that letter, my dear. Don't you touch it, mind.'

As she spoke she thrust the note between the leaves, and then walked into the shop with her niece, and placed the book upon a shelf.

'There, if you behave yourself you shall see who buys those poems; but, once more, never a word to a soul.'

'Oh, no, auntie, never,' said the girl, with her big eyes rolling. 'But oh, I say, auntie, isn't it fun?'

'Isn't what fun?'

'I know,' giggled the girl; 'there was a letter in that card-case you sold. I saw you put it there.'

'Well, well, perhaps there was, my dear. I must oblige customers, and the profits on things are so small, and rents so high. We must live, you see. And now mind this: if Mrs. Frank Burnett comes, you call me.'

'Couldn't I sell her that volume of poems, auntie?' said the girl eagerly.

'No, certainly not; and now look here, miss. Don't you ever pretend to be simple any more.'

'No, auntie,' said the girl, 'I won't;' and she drew her
breath thickly and gave a smack with her lips, as if she
were tasting something very nice.

Loungers dropped in, and loungers dropped out, coming
for the most part to meet other loungers, and, like the
Athenians of old, to ask whether there was anything new.
Sometimes Miss Clode was consulted, and when this was
the case, her way was soft, deprecating, and diffident. She
thought she had heard this; she believed that she had heard
that; she would endeavour to find out; or, yes, to be sure,
her ladyship was right: it was so, she remembered now.
While when not invited to give opinions, she was busy in
the extreme over some item connected with her business,
and hearing and seeing nothing, with that bended head so
intent upon arranging, or booking, or tying up.

There was very little, though, that Miss Clode did not
hear, especially when some one of a group said, 'Oh, fie !'
or 'No, really, now !' or 'How shocking !' and there was a
little burst of giggles.

In due time, just as Miss Clode was instructing her niece
in the art of tying up a packet of wools, so that one end was
left open and the dealer could see at a glance what colours
it contained, Annie's jaw dropped, and seemed to draw down
the lower lids of her eyes, so that they were opened to the
fullest extent, for Frank Burnett's handsome britzka drew
up at the door, the steps were rattled down, *flip, flop, flap,*

with a vigorous action that would bring people to the windows to see, and, all sweetness in appearance and odour, like the blossom she was, the M.C.'s idol stepped daintily rustling down, the very model of all that was *naïve* and girlish.

'Who'd ever think she was a wife?' said Miss Clode to herself.

'Oh my! isn't she pretty?' said Annie.

'Go on tying up those packets, and don't take any notice,' said Miss Clode; and then, with the greatest of deference, wished her visitor good-morning, and begged to know how she was.

'Not very well, Miss Clode: so tired. Society is so exacting. Can you recommend me any book that will distract me a little?'

'Let me see, ma'am,' said Miss Clode, turning her head on one side in a very bird-like way, and bending forward as if she were going to peck a seed off the counter.

'Something that will really take me out of myself.'

'The last romance might be too exciting, ma'am?'

'Do you think it would?'

'Ye-e-e-es. Oh, yes, decidedly so in your case, ma'am,' said Miss Clode, in quite the tone of a female physician. 'Poems—soft, dreamy, soothing poems, now, would I think be most suited.'

'Oh, do you think so?' said Mrs. Burnett half pettishly.

'Yes, ma'am, I have a volume here, not included in the library, but for sale—"Lays of the Heart-strings"—by a gentleman of quality. I should recommend it strongly.'

'Oh, dear no,' exclaimed the visitor, as Miss Clode took the work from the shelf. 'I don't think a—well, I will look at it,' she said, blushing vividly, as she saw that the book did not thoroughly close in one part. 'Perhaps you are right, Miss Clode. I will take it. What is the price?'

'Half a guinea, ma'am, to subscribers, and I will call you a subscriber. Shall I do it up in paper?'

'Yes, by all means. What delightful weather we are having!'

'Delightful, indeed, ma'am,' said Miss Clode, whose face was simply business-like. There was not a nerve-twitch, not a peculiar glance to indicate that she was playing a double part; and it was wonderfully convenient. Visitors, both ladies and gentlemen, liked it immensely, and patronized her accordingly, for no Artesian well was ever so deep and dark as Miss Clode, or as silent. She knew absolutely nothing. Mrs. Frank Burnett had bought a volume of poems at her establishment, that was all. Anybody might have slipped the note inside. While as to seeking a client's confidence, or alluding in the mildest way to any little transaction that had taken place for the sake of obtaining further fee or reward, any client would have told you that with the purchase of book, album, card-case, or needle-housewife, every transaction was at an end; and so Miss Clode's business throve, and Lord Carboro' called her the Saltinville sphinx.

'Is there any particular news stirring, Miss Clode?'

'Really, no, ma'am,' said that lady, pausing in the act of cutting the twine that confined the book. 'A new family has come to the George; and, by the way, I have to send their cards to Mr. Denville.'

'Oh, of course, I don't want to know anything about that,' said Mrs. Burnett hastily.

'The officers are talking of getting up a ball before long, and they say that a certain person will be there.'

'Indeed!' said the visitor, flushing.

'Yes, ma'am, I was told so, and—ahem!—here is Lord Carboro'. Half a guinea, ma'am, if you please.'

Surely there was no occasion for a lady to look so flushed in the act of extricating a little gold coin from her purse; but somehow the ordinary sweet ingenuous look would not come back to May Burnett's face, any more than the coin would consent to come out of the little, long net purse with gold tassels and slides; and the colour deepened as the keen little eyes of the old man settled for a moment on the tied-up book, and then on Miss Clode's face.

'What an old sphinx it is,' he thought to himself. 'The day grows brighter every hour, Mrs. Burnett,' he said gallantly. 'It has culminated in the sight of you.'

'Your lordship's compliments are overpowering,' said the lady, with a profound curtsey; and then she secured her book and would have fled, but his lordship insisted upon escorting her to her carriage, hat in hand, and he cursed that new pomade in a way that was silent but not divine, for it lifted one side of his hair as if he were being scalped when he raised his hat.

'Good-morning, good-morning!' he said, as the carriage drove off. 'Little wretch,' he muttered as he watched the equipage out of sight, but with his hat on now. 'I hate scandal, but if we don't have a toothsome bit before long over that little woman, I'm no man. It's vexatious, too,' he said angrily, 'doosid vexatious. I don't like it. So different to the other, and our sweet Christians here will throw dirt at both. Can't help it; can't help it. Well, Miss Clode, anything you want to recommend to me?'

'Yes, my lord, I have a very charming little tortoiseshell-covered engagement-book or two. Most elegant and very cheap.'

'I don't want cheap things, my dear little woman. Let me see, let me see. Oh, yes, very nice indeed,' he said, opening the case, and letting a scented note drop out on the counter. 'Same make, I see, as the cigar-case I bought last week.'

'No, my lord, it is French.'

'No, no—no, no; don't tell me—English, English. People

have stuck their advertisement in. Send it back to 'em. Do for some one else.'

'Then your lordship does not like the case?'

'My dear little woman, but I do, doosidly, but don't offer me any more with that person's circular inside. There, there, there; take the price out of that five-pound note. Two guineas? And very cheap too. Doosid pretty little piece of art, Miss Clode. Doosid pretty little piece of art.'

'Wouldn't he have old Mrs. Dean's pink note, auntie?' said Annie, as soon as his lordship had gone.

'My dear child, this will never do. You see and hear far too much.'

'Please auntie, I can't help it,' drawled the girl. 'I shouldn't speak like that to anyone else.'

'Ah, well, I suppose not; and I have done right, I see. No; he would not have the pink note. This is the second he has refused. Old Mrs. Dean will be furious, but she must have known that it would not last long.'

'I know why it is,' said Annie eagerly. 'I know, auntie.'

'You know, child?'

'Yes, auntie; old Lord——'

'Hush! don't call people old.'

'Lord Carboro' has taken a fancy to some one else.'

'Well, perhaps so,' said Miss Clode, tapping her niece's fat cheek, and smiling. 'People do take fancies, even when they are growing older,' she added with a sigh. 'Well, he hasn't taken a fancy to you.'

'Ugh! Oh, gracious, auntie, don't,' said the girl with a shudder. 'He's such a horrid old man. I can't think how it was that beautiful Miss Cora Dean could like him.'

'I can,' said Miss Clode shortly. 'Now go and see about the dinner, and don't talk so much.'

CHAPTER XVI.

MRS. DEAN'S DRIVE.

MAY BURNETT, with her little palpitating heart full of trouble, pretty butterfly of fashion that she was, was flitting through the sunshine one afternoon for the second time to confide her troublesome secret to her sister and obtain her help, but her heart failed her again. The right road was so steep and hard, so she turned down the wrong one once more, laughed at Claire, and left her with saddened face, as in response to the again-repeated question, 'Why did you come?' she replied:

'Oh, I don't know. Just to try and make people forget what a horrible house this has been. I almost wonder, though, that I dare to call.'

She gave her sister a child-like kiss, and away she went full sail, and with no more ballast than she possessed two years before, at the time she was so severely taken to task for flirting with Louis Gravani, when the handsome young artist painted her portrait and that of her father, hers to

hang in the drawing-room, that of the Master of the Ceremonies in the ante-room at the Assembly Rooms.

Claire went to the window to gaze down over the flowers
in the balcony at her sister, as she stepped lightly into her
carriage, just as manly, handsome Richard Linnell came by
on the other side, to raise his hat gravely to each of the
sisters in turn, with the effect of making Claire shrink back
more into the room, so that she only heard the door of the
britzka banged to, and the horses start off, while Richard
Linnell went on with bended head and knitted brows,
thinking of the part he had taken in the serenade on that
terrible night.

'Goose!' said May Burnett to herself angrily, as she
ordered the footman to go to Miss Clode's. 'I believe she'd
be ready to throw herself away on that penniless fellow. I
haven't patience with her, and——'

Here she had to bend to a couple of ladies with a most
gracious smile. A few yards further and she encountered
Lord Carboro', whose hat was carefully raised to her, and
on turning the bend where the cliff curved off to the north,
she came suddenly upon a handsome pony carriage, driven
by Cora Dean in a dazzling new costume of creamy silk and
lace, while her mother leaned back in ruby satin, with her
eyes half closed, a small groom behind, seated upon a very
tiny perch, having his arms closely folded, and his hat cocked
at a wonderful angle.

The driver of the high-stepping pair of ponies stared hard at May Burnett, while that lady leaned back languidly, and quite ignored the presence of the handsome actress.

'Little upstart!' muttered Cora, as she gave her ponies a sharp cut, making them tear along. 'I'm not good enough for her to even see; but maybe smuts will fall on the whitest snow. Who knows, my pretty baby madam? Get on with you then!'

Whish-swish, and the ponies sent the chalky dust flying as they tore along.

'Now, lookye here, Betsy, once for all,' said Mrs. Dean angrily; 'if you are going to drive like that, I stay at home. I like my bones, though they do ache sometimes, and I'm not going to have them broke to please you.'

Cora frowned, and softly took up the second rein with the effect of checking the ponies' rattling gallop just as heads were being turned and gentlemen on horseback were starting off in pursuit.

'I ain't easily frightened, Betsy, you know,' said Mrs. Dean, panting. 'Speaking as a woman as has faced a whole company in the bad days on treasury night, when there's been nothing in the cash-box, and your poor father off his head, I say I ain't easily frightened.'

'Now, mother—I mean mamma—how are we to get into society if you will refer so constantly to those wretched old days?'

' They weren't wretched old days, my dear, and I was a deal happier then than I am now. But never mind; we've got our tickets. I knew old Denville would get 'em, and my Betsy 'll startle some of 'em at the ball, I know. Hold 'em in tighter, my dear, do.'

' Don't be so foolishly nervous, mother. I have them well in hand.'

' But why does that one keep laying down its ears and squeaking, and trying to bite t'other one?'

' Play,' said Cora shortly.

' Then I wish he'd play in the stable, and behave himself when he comes out on the cliff. My word, look at that old Drelincourt, Bet—Cora,' said the old woman, giving her daughter a nudge. ' Look at the nasty old thing in black. If she'd had any decency, she'd have left the place when her old sister was killed, instead of being pushed about in her chair like that.'

' But she has a house here of her own,' said Cora shortly, as she guided her ponies in and out among the fashionable equipages, not one of whose lady occupants noticed her.

' Look at 'em,' whispered Mrs. Dean, nudging her daughter again. ' They're a-busting with envy, but they shall be civil to you yet. I did grudge the money for the turn out, and I told Ashley it was a swindle, but they do show off, and I'm glad I bought 'em. Look at the fine madams in that broosh; they're as envious as can be. Hit 'm up, Cora, and make 'em go. I should like to see anybody else's gal with such a turn-out.'

Too showy, and with a suspicion of the circus in the style of the harness and the colours of the rosettes; but Cora Dean's pony carriage, driven as it was in masterly style, created no little sensation in Saltinville; and if, in addition to the salutes of the gentlemen, which she acknowledged very superciliously, only one lady would have bowed in recognition, Cora Dean would have enjoyed her drive, and probably have gone more slowly.

As it was, in obedience to her mother's nudges and admonitions to 'Hit 'm up again,' she gave the ponies flick after flick with the whip, and increased the restiveness consequent upon plenty of spirit and too much corn.

It was a risky drive with restive beasts along that cliff with so slight a railing, and the archives of the town told how one Sir Rumble Thornton had gone over with his curricle and pair on to the shingle below, to be killed with his horses. But Cora Dean and her mother thought only of making a show, and the well-bred little ponies seemed to be kept thoroughly in hand by their mistress, though they were fretting and champing their bits and sending flakes of foam all over their satin coats.

'I'm getting used to it now, Cora, my dear,' panted the old woman. 'I don't feel so squirmy inside, and as if I should be obliged to go home for a drop of brandy. Humph! I wish you wouldn't bow to him.'

'Why not? He's our neighbour,' said Cora tartly, as Richard Linnell took off his hat. 'He's the most thorough gentleman in this town.'

'P'raps he is, but I don't think anything of such gentlemen as he is—now Betsy, do a' done. Don't drive like that. I was getting used to it, but now you've made my pore 'art fly up into my mouth.'

A sharp snatch at the reins had made the ponies rear up, and Richard Linnell, who was looking after them, started to go to Cora's help, but a cut of the whip sent the two ponies on again, and the carriage spun along, past the wide opening to the pier, down which Richard Linnell turned to think out how he might get over the prejudice he knew that Mr. Denville had against him, and to wonder why Claire had grown so cold and strange.

'I am getting well used to it now, Betsy,' said Mrs. Dean, as they drove right along the London road for a mile or two; 'but, I say, hadn't you better turn their heads now? Let's get back on the cliff, where they can see us. I hate these fields and hedges. Let's go back by the other road, down by Lord Carboro's house, and through the street down to the pier.'

'Very well,' said Cora shortly; and she turned the ponies, and took the upper road.

Now, it so happened that after a short promenade Lord Carboro' had found out that it was going to rain, by a double barometer which he carried in his boots.

'Confound these corns!' he grumbled. 'Ah, Barclay,' he cried to a thick-set man whom he met at that moment, 'collecting your dues? It's going to rain.'

'Yes, my lord. My corns shoot horribly.'

'So do mine; doosid bad. I'm going to get the carriage and have a drive. Can't walk.'

He nodded and went back to his handsome house and grounds, contenting himself with sitting down in the lodge portico while the gardener's wife ordered the carriage to be got ready.

'It isn't handsome, but it suits me,' his lordship used to say, 'and it's comfortable. If I can't have things as I like with my money, and at my time of life, why it's doosid strange.'

So he waited till a groom brought the carriage down the drive, and then looked at it as it came.

'Don't do to go wooing in,' he said, with a chuckle, as he got in and took the reins; and certainly it did not look like the chariot of love, for it was a little, low basket carriage, big enough to hold one, and shaped very much like a bath-chair. It was drawn by a very large, grey, well-clipped donkey with enormous ears, quite an aristocrat of his race, with his well-filled skin and carefully blackened harness.

'Thankye, John. Thankye, Mrs. Roberts,' said his lordship, as he shook the reins. 'Go on, Balaam.'

Balaam went deliberately on, and just as they were going out of the great iron gates, and his lordship was indulging in a pinch of snuff, there was the rattle of wheels to his right, and Cora Dean came along with her ponies at a smart trot, her mother looking like an over-blown peony by her side.

'Juno, by Jove!' said his lordship, preparing to raise his hat.

But just then—it was a matter of moments—Balaam stood stock still, drew his great flap ears forward and pointed them at the ponies, and staring hard, lifted his tail, and, showing his teeth, uttered with outstretched neck a most discordant roaring—*Hee-haw—Hee-haw !*

Cora's ponies stopped short, trembling and snorting. Then, with a jerk that threatened to snap the harness, and as if moved by the same impulse, they plunged forward and tore down the road that, a hundred yards further on, became busy street, and went down at a sharp angle right for the pier.

'Betsy !' shouted Mrs. Dean.

Cora sat firm as a rock, and caught up the second rein to pull heavily on the curb, when—*snap !*—the rein parted at the buckle, and with only the regular snaffle rein to check the headlong gallop, the driver dragged in vain.

The road became street almost like a flash ; the street with its busy shops seemed to rush by the carriage ; a bath-chair at a shop door, fortunately empty, was caught, in spite of Cora's efforts to guide the ponies, and smashed to atoms, the flying pieces and the noise maddening the ponies in their headlong race.

It was a steep descent, too, and with such bits even a man's arm could not have restrained the fiery little animals as they tore on straight for the sea.

'By Jove !' panted Lord Carboro', jumping out of his little carriage, and, forgetful of all infirmities, he began to run ; 'they'll be over the cliff. No, by all that's horrible, they'll go right down the pier !'

CHAPTER XVII.

RICHARD LINNELL was very blind as he walked down the pier, stopping here and there to lay his hand upon the slight rail, and watch the changing colours on the sea, which was here one dazzling sheen of silver, there stained with shade after shade of glorious blue, borrowed from the sky, which was as smiling now as it was tearful but a few days back, when it was clouded over with gloom.

Then he gazed wistfully at a mackerel boat that could not get in for want of wind, and lay with its mast describing arcs on the ether, while its brown sails kept filling out and flapping, and then hanging empty from the spars.

It was a glorious day; one that should have filled all young and buoyant hearts with hope, but Richard Linnell's was not buoyant, for it felt heavy as lead.

He told himself that he loved Claire Denville truly a man could love; and time back she had been ready to respond to his bows; her eyes, too, had seemed to look brightly upon him ; but since that dreadful night when he had been deluded into making one of the half-tipsy party gathered beneath her window, and had played that serenade, all had been changed.

It was horrible ! Such a night as that, when, judging from what he could glean, the agony and trouble of father and daughter must have been unbearable. And yet he had been there like some contemptible street musician playing beneath her window, and she must know it was he.

That white hand that opened the window and waved them away was not hers, though, but old Denville's, and that was the only relief he found.

He was very blind, or he would have seen more than one pair of eyes brighten as he sauntered down the pier, and more than one fan flutter as he drew near, and its owner prepare to return his bow while he passed on with his eyes mentally closed.

He was very blind, for he did not see one of the attractive ladies, nor one of those who tried to be attractive as he dawdled on, thinking of the face that appeared, somehow, among the flowers at Claire Denville's window ; then of pretty little blossom-like May Burnett, who people said was so light and frivolous.

Then he asked himself why he was frittering away his life in Saltinville with his father instead of taking to some manly career, and making for himself a name.

' Because I'm chained,' he said, half aloud, as he returned
a couple of salutes from Sir Harry Payne and Sir Matthew
Bray—rather coldly given, condescending salutations that
brought a curl of contempt to his lip.

These gentlemen were near the end of the pier, and he
passed them, and went on to look out to sea on the other
side, where a swarthy-looking man was wading nearly to
his arm-pits, and pushing a pole before him, while a creel
hung upon his back.

' I tell you what,' said a loud voice, ' let's go back now,
Josiah, and wait till he comes ashore, and then you can buy
a pint o' the live s'rimps, and I'll see them boiled myself.'

' No, no.   Here's Major Rockley,' said the speaker's companion, Josiah Barclay, twitching his heavy brows.   ' He
wants to see me about some money.   Why he looks as if
he was going to buy shrimps himself.   How do, Mr. Linnell !'

Richard bowed to the thick-set busy-looking man, and to
his pleasant-faced plump lady, who smiled at him in turn,
and then passed on, walking back and passing the Major,
who did not see him, but watched the fisherman as he
lifted his net, picked out the shrimps, shook it, and plunged
it in again to wade on through the calm water, and pushing
it before him as he went.

There were other looks directed at the handsome young
fellow, who seemed so unconscious, and so great a contrast
to the bucks and beaux who were waving clouded canes,

taking snuff from gold boxes, and standing in groups in studied attitudes.

Even Lady Drelincourt in her deep mourning, and with a precaution taken against any further mishap to her pet, in the shape of a delicately thin plated chain, smiled as Richard Linnell drew near, and waited for an admiring glance and a bow, and when they did not come, said ' Boor !' half audibly and closed her fan with a snap.

' Beg pardon, m'lady,' said the tall footman.

' Turn the chair and go back.'

The tall footman in black, with the great plaited worsted aiguillettes looped so gracefully up to the buttons on his breast, did not turn the chair, but turned round and stared with parted lips and a look of bewildered horror towards the shore end of the pier, from whence came all at once a rushing sound, shrieks, cries, and then the rapid beating of horses' feet, sounding hollow upon the boards, and the whirr of wheels.

' Take care !'

' Run !'

' Keep to the side !'

' No. Get to the end.'

There was a rush and confusion. Ladies shrieked and fainted. Gentlemen ran to their help, or ran to their own help to get out of the way. Sir Harry Payne and his friend climbed over the railing and stood outside on the edge of the pier, holding on to the bar to avoid a fall into the water. Major Rockley did likewise on the other side, and all the while the rush, the trampling, and the hollow sound increased.

It was only a matter of moments. Cora Dean's handsome ponies had not gone right over the cliff; but in response to a desperate tug at the reins given by their driver, had swerved a little and dashed through the pier gateway, and then the loungers saw the beautiful woman, with her lips compressed, sitting upright, pulling at the reins with both hands, while her mother in her rich satin dress crouched down with her eyes shut and her full florid face horribly mottled with white.

It was a case of *sauve qui peut* for the most part, as the frantic ponies, growing more frightened by the shouts and cries and the hollow beating of their hoofs, tore on to what seemed to be certain death.

'Here, old girl, quick, down here!' cried Barclay, as he saw the coming danger; and he thrust his trembling wife into one of the embayments at the side of the pier, where there was a shelter for the look-out men and the materials for trimming the pier-lights were kept. 'Bravo! bravo, lad!' he cried hoarsely, as he saw Richard Linnell dash forward, and, at the imminent peril of his life, snatch at the bearing rein of one of the ponies, catch hold and hang to it, as the force with which the animals were galloping on took him off his legs.

It was a score of yards from Barclay, who was going to
his aid when the rein broke, and Richard Linnell fell and
rolled over and over to strike against a group of shrieking
women clinging to the side railings. The ponies tore on
past Barclay, whose well-meant efforts to check them were
vain, and before the danger could be thoroughly realized
Cora Dean's little steeds had blindly rushed at the rotting
railings at the end of the pier, and gone through them.
There was a hoarse, wild shriek from half a hundred voices,
a crash, a plunge, and ponies, carriage, and the occupants
were in the sea.

'A boat!'

'The life-buoy!'

'Ropes here, quick.'

'Help!—help!'

Cries; the rush of a crowd to the end of the pier.

A very Babel of confusion, in the midst of which a man
was seen to plunge off the end of the pier and swim towards
where Cora Dean could be seen clinging to the broad splash-
board of the carriage, drawn through the water, while, after
rising from their plunge, the ponies swam together for a few
moments, and then began to snort and plunge, and were
rapidly drowning each other.

'Oh, horrid, horrid, horrid!' cried a woman's voice.
'Help! help! Josiah, come back! He'll be drowned!'

For Josiah Barclay had seized a life-buoy, and throwing

off his coat, boldly plunged in after the first man had set an example.

' A good job if he is,' muttered Sir Matthew Bray—a kindly wish echoed by several lookers-on who thought of certain slips of paper (stamped) that the money-lender had in his cash-box at home.

But Josiah Barclay did not find a fair amount of stoutness interfere with his floating powers, as he held on to the life-buoy with one hand, swimming with the other towards what looked like a patch of red in the sea, surrounding a white face; and a roar of cheers rose from the crowd who were watching him as he reached Mrs. Dean, who had rolled from the carriage, and now gripped the life-buoy as it was pushed towards her, and fainted away.

But the majority were watching the daring man who was striving after the ponies, which were now about fifty yards from the pier, and instead of swimming away, pawing the water frantically, so that the end of the accident seemed near.

Boats were putting off from the shore, but it would be long enough before they could do any good. The chances were that the end would have come before they reached the spot, and Richard Linnell was now within half a dozen yards.

' Let go,' he shouted to Cora. ' Try and throw yourself out this side, and I'll get you ashore.'

She only turned a dazed, despairing look in his direction,

too much paralyzed by the horror of her situation to even grasp his meaning.

'All right, Master Linnell, sir,' growled a deep voice. 'Take it coolly, and we'll do it.'

Linnell glanced aside, and saw that the swarthy fisherman who had been shrimping was not a couple of yards behind him.

'Look ye here, sir. Let the lady be. I'll go round t'other side. You go this. Mind they don't kick you. Take care. Wo-ho, my pretties; wo-ho, my lads,' he cried to the ponies, as, perfectly at his ease in the water, he swam past their heads, well clear of their beating and pawing hoofs, and got to the other side.

In cases of emergency, whether the order be right or wrong, one that is given by a firm, cool man is generally obeyed, and it was so here, for Linnell took a stroke or two forward towards the off-side pony, leaving Cora clinging to the front of the little carriage.

'Wo-ho, my beauties. Steady, boys,' cried the big fisherman soothingly.

'Woa, lad, woa, then,' cried Linnell, in imitation of his companion.

The ponies, the moment before snorting and plunging desperately, seemed to gather encouragement from the voices, and ceasing their frantic efforts, allowed themselves to sink lower in the water, let their bits be seized, and with outstretched necks, and nostrils just clear of the water, began to swim steadily and well.

'That's it, lads, steady it is!' cried the fisherman. 'Lay out well clear of 'em, Master Linnell, sir. Mind they don't kick you. I'll steer 'em, and we shall do it. You hold on, mum; it's all right.'

Cora's head and shoulders were above the water and the ponies were swimming well now, and obeying the pressure of the fisherman's hand, though they needed little guidance now they were making steadily for the shore.

'I thought they'd do it, Master Linnell, sir. Good boys, then. Good lads. Pity to let 'em drown,' said the fisherman coolly.

'Right,' cried Linnell, easing the pony on his side by swimming with one hand. 'Keep still, Miss Dean. We shall soon be ashore. There's no danger now. Yes, there is,' he muttered. 'Those boats.'

Cora turned her eyes upon him with a frightened look, but she was growing more calm, though she could not speak, and the ponies kept on snorting loudly as they swam on.

'Keep quiet, will you, you fools!' grumbled Dick Miggles, as bursts of cheers kept rising from the pier, answered by a gathering crowd on the beach about where they were expected to land, while the cliff was now lined with people who had heard of the accident on the pier.

'Here! hoy!' roared Dick Miggles, who had grasped the danger. 'Wo-ho, my boys, I'm with you. It's all right.'

'Ahoy!' came from the nearest boat, whose occupants were rowing with all their might.

'Back with you. D'ye hear! Wo-ho, lads; it's all right. Back, I say. You'll frighten the horses again.'

'We're coming to help you,' came from the boat.

'Go back, curse yer!' roared Dick. 'Don't you see what you're doing.'

The ponies were getting scared by the shouting, but by dint of patting and soothing words, they were calmed down once more, and the boatmen, in obedience to the orders given, ceased rowing.

'Go back, and bid 'em hold their row,' cried Dick, as he guided the ponies. 'We must get in quiet, or the horses 'll go mad again.'

The men rowed back, communicating their orders to the other boats, whose occupants rested on their oars, while, like some sea-queen, Cora was drawn on in her chariot towards the shore, but looking terribly unaccustomed to the mode of procedure, as she still clung to the front of the little carriage.

'Miggles.'

''Ullo?'

'Can you manage them alone? The lady.'

' All right, Master Linnell, sir. They'll go now. We shall be ashore directly.'

He had turned his head and seen what was wrong as Richard Linnell loosed his hold of the pony's head, letting it swim on, though the frightened beast uttered a snorting neigh and tried to follow him, till its attention was taken up by the soothing words of Dick Miggles, and it struck out afresh for the shore.

Meanwhile Richard had caught Cora Dean as she loosened her grasp of the front of the carriage, for he had seen that something was coming as her countenance changed and her eyes half closed.

It was an easy task, for he had only to check her as she was floating out of the carriage, and take hold of the front with his right hand to let himself be drawn ashore.

She opened her eyes again with a start, as if she were making an effort to master her emotion, and they rested on Linnell's as he held her tightly to his breast. Then she shivered and clung to him, and the next minute the ponies' hoofs touched the shingly bottom, and people began to realize how it was that the carriage had not sunk in the deep water and dragged the ponies down.

It was plain enough. There was nothing but the slight body with its seats, which had been torn from springs, axle-trees, and wheels, giving it more than ever the aspect of a chariot drawn by sea-horses through the waves.

The ponies were for making a fresh dash as soon as they felt the yielding shingle beneath their hoofs, but a dozen willing hands were at their heads ; the remains of the carriage were drawn up the beach, and the traces were loosened and twisted up, while Cora was borne by a couple of gentlemen to one of several carriages offered to bear her home.

As for Linnell, he was surrounded by an excited crowd of people eager to shake hands with him, but none of whom could answer his questions about Mrs. Dean.

' Mrs. Dean ?' said a wet, thick-set man, elbowing his way through. ' All right ; sent home in Lord Carboro's donkey-carriage. Mr. Linnell, sir, your hand, sir. God bless you, sir, for a brave gentleman ! Nice pair of wet ones, aren't we ?'

' Oh, never mind, Mr. Barclay,' cried Linnell, shaking hands. ' I'm only too thankful that we have got them safe ashore.'

' With no more harm done than to give the coachbuilder a job, eh ? Ha, ha !'

' Three cheers for 'em !' shouted a voice ; and they were heartily given.

' And three more for Fisherman Dick !' cried Linnell.

' Don't, Master Richard, sir—please don't !' cried the swarthy fisherman modestly.

' He did more than I did.'

'No, no, Master Richard, sir,' protested Dick, as the cheers were heartily given; and then a horrible thought smote Linnell:

'The boy—Mrs. Dean's little groom! Where is he?'

'Oh, I'm all right, sir,' cried a shrill voice. 'When I see as missus couldn't stop the ponies, I dropped down off my seat on to the pier.'

'Hurray! Well done, youngster!' cried first one and then another.

'Look here, Mr. Richard,' cried Barclay; 'my place is nearest; come there, and send for some dry clothes.'

'No, no; I'll get back,' said Linnell. 'Thanks all the same. Let me pass, please;' and as Cora Dean's ponies were led off to their stable, and Barclay went towards where plump Mrs. Barclay was signalling him on the cliff, the young man hurried off homeward, followed by bursts of cheers, and having hard work to escape from the many idlers who were eager to shake his hand.

CHAPTER XVIII.

UNREASONABLE CHILDREN.

' CLAIRE, Claire !   Quick, Claire !'

Pale and very anxious of aspect, Claire hurried down from her room, to find her father, in his elaborate costume, standing in an attitude before one of the mirrors, not heeding her, so wrapped was he in his thoughts.

Her brow contracted, and she looked at him wonderingly, asking herself was his memory going, or was something more terrible than the loss of memory coming on ? for he appeared to have forgotten that which was an agony to her, night and day.

Something had happened to please him, she knew, for his countenance at such times was easy to read ; but all the same, his worn aspect was pitiable, and it was plain that beneath the mask he wore the terrible care was working its way.

' What is it, papa ?' she said, in the calm, sad way which had become habitual with her.

' What is it ?' he cried, in his mincing, artificial style.

11—2

'Success! Assured fortune! The wretched fribbles who have been disposed to slight me and refuse my offices will now be at my feet. A brilliant match for you, and a high position in the world of fashion.'

'Father!'

'Hush, child, and listen. The position of both of you is assured; a peaceful and more prosperous fortune for me! The few trifles I ask for: my snuff, a glass of port—one only—my cutlet, a suit of clothes when I desire a change, without an insulting reference to an old bill, the deference of tradespeople, freedom from debt. Claire, at last, at last!'

'Oh, papa!' cried the girl, with the tears welling over and dropping slowly from her beautiful eyes, while her sweet mouth seemed all a-tremble, and her agitated hands were stretched out to clasp the old man's arm.

But he waved her off.

'Don't, don't, Claire,' he said quickly. 'See there. I do detest to have my coat spotted. It is so foolish and weak.'

Claire smiled—a sweet, sad smile—as she drew a clean cambric handkerchief from the pocket of her apron, shook it out, showing a long slit and a series of careful darns, removed the pearly drop before it had time to soak the cloth, and exclaimed:

'Then the town has conferred a salary upon you?'

'Pah! As if I would condescend to take it, girl!' cried the old man, drawing himself up more stiffly.

' A legacy ?'

The Master of the Ceremonies shook his head.

' A commission for Morton ?'

' No, no, no.'

' Then——'

The old man waved his cane with a graceful flourish, placed it in the hand that held his snuff-box, opened the latter, and, after tapping it, took a pinch, as if it were a matter calling forth long study of deportment to perform, closed the box with a loud snap, and said, in a haughty, affected tone :

' Half an hour since, on a well-filled parade, I encountered His Royal Highness and a group of friends.'

He paused, and took out a silk handkerchief, embroidered here and there with purple flowers by his child.

' And then——'

There was a flourish of the handkerchief, and the flicking away of imaginary specks from the tightly-buttoned coat.

' His Royal Highness——'

' Yes, papa,' said Claire piteously, as he looked at her as if asking her attention.

At that moment Morton entered, looking weary and discontented ; but, seeing his father's peculiar look, he checked the words he was about to say, and watched his face as he gave his handkerchief another flourish, replaced it, and took his cane from his left hand to twirl it gracefully.

' His Royal Highness shook hands with me.'

' Oh !' exclaimed Morton, while Claire's brow grew more rugged.

' Shook hands with you, father ?' said Morton eagerly.

' And asked me for a pinch of snuff.'

There was a dead silence in the room as Claire clasped her hands together and trembled, and seemed about to speak, but dared not; while Morton screwed up his mouth to whistle, but refrained, looking half contemptuously at his father the while.

' Fortune has thrown a magnificent chance in our way.'

' I say, dad, what do you mean with your magnificent chance ?'

' I have hopes, too, for Claire. I cannot say much yet, but I have great hopes,' he continued, ignoring the question of his son.

' Oh, papa !'

' Yes, my child, I have. I can say no more now, but I have hopes.'

Claire's careworn face grew more cloudy as she uttered a low sigh.

' But look here, father ; what do you mean,' repeated Morton, ' by your magnificent chance ?'

The Master of the Ceremonies coughed behind one delicate hand, brushed a few imaginary specks from his sleeve,

then took out his snuff-box, and refreshed himself with a
pinch in a very elaborate way.

'You are a man now, Morton, and I will speak plainly to
you, as I have before now spoken plainly to your sisters.
My only hope for the future is to see you both make good
marriages.'

'Why, that won't send you to heaven, father,' said the
lad, grinning.

'I mean my—our—earthly future, sir,' said the old man.
'This is no time for ribald jest. Remember your duty to
me, sir, and follow out my wishes.'

'Oh, very well, father,' said Morton sulkily.

'But, papa dear, you surely do not think of Morton marry-
ing,' said Claire anxiously.

'And why not, madam, pray? Younger men have
married before now, even princes and kings, when it was
politically necessary, at twelve and fifteen; my memory
does not serve me at the moment for names, but let that
pass.'

'But have you any fixed ideas upon the subject, papa?'

'My dear Claire! How dense you are! Did I not tell
you about Morton's providential rescue of Lady Drelincourt's favourite, and of her impassioned admiration of his
bravery? She saw him at great disadvantage then; but I
am going to arrange with—er—one of the principal tailors,
and Morton must now take his place amongst the best

dressed bucks on the Parade. With his manly young person, and a few touches in deportment that I can give him, his prospect is sure, I will answer for it.'

'Ha—ha—ha—ha—ha—ha!' roared Morton, bursting out into a fit of uncontrollable laughter.

'Morton!' and the old man turned round fiercely.

'Why, you don't want me to marry that old female Guy Fawkes, father!'

'Morton! my son! you grieve and pain me. How dare you speak like that of a leader of society—a lady of title, sir —of great wealth. Why, her diamonds are magnificent. will be plain with you. You have only to play your cards well, and in due course others will be issued—Mr. Morton Denville and the Countess of Drelincourt.'

'Why, father, all the fellows would laugh at me.'

'Sir, a man with horses, carriages, servants, a town mansion and country seat, and a large income can laugh at the world.'

'Oh, yes, of course, father; but she's fifty or sixty, and I'm not twenty.'

'What has that to do with it, sir! How often do men of sixty marry girls of seventeen, eighteen, and nineteen?'

'But she paints, and wears false hair.'

'Matters of which every gentleman, sir, would be profoundly ignorant as regards a lady of title.'

'But, papa dear, surely you are not serious?' said Claire, who had listened with horror painted in every feature.

'I was never more serious in my life, child. Lady Drelincourt is not young, but she is a most amiable woman, with no other weakness than a love for play.'

'And little beasts of dogs,' said Morton contemptuously.

'Of course, because there is a void in her womanly heart. That void, my son, you must try and fill.'

'Oh, nonsense, father!'

'Nonsense! Morton, are you mad? Are you going to throw away a fortune, and a great position in society? Of course, I do not say that such an event will follow, but it is time you began to assert your position. You did well the other day on the pier.'

'Yes,' said Morton with a sneer. 'I fished out a d g. Now Dick Linnell did something worth——'

'Silence, sir! Do not mention his name in my presence, I beg,' said the old man sternly; and he left the house.

'Well, I tell you what it is, Sis,' said Morton, speaking from the window, where he had gone to see his father mince by, 'the old dad hasn't been right since that night. I think he's going off his head.'

There was no reply, and, turning round, it was to find that he was alone, for Claire, unable to bear the strain longer, had glided from the room.

CHAPTER XIX.

MISS CLODE'S HERO.

No one would have called Miss Clode pretty, 'but there were traces,' as the Master of the Ceremonies said. She was thin and middle-aged now, but she had once been a very charming woman; and, though the proprietress of the circulating library at Saltinville, a keen observer would have said that she was a lady.

Richard Linnell entered her shop on the morning after the carriage accident, and a curious flush came into her little thin face. There was a light in her eye that seemed to make the worn, jaded face pleasanter to look upon, and it seemed as if something of the little faded woman's true nature was peeping out.

She did not look like the little go-between in scores of flirtations and intrigues; but as if the natural love of her nature had come to the surface, from where it generally lay latent, and her eyes seemed to say:

'Ah, if I could have married, and had a son like that.'

It is the fashion, nowadays, for ladies to attempt a strong-minded *rôle*, and profess to despise the tyrant man; to take to college life and professorship; to cry aloud and shout for woman's rights and independence; for votes and the entry to the school board, vestry, and the Parliamentary bench; when all the time Nature says in her gentle but inflexible way: 'Foolish women; it was not for these things that you were made to tread the earth.'

Study! Yes, nothing is too abtruse, nowadays. The pretty maidens, who used to learn a little French with their music and drawing, now take to Greek and Latin and the higher mathematics, but they cannot stitch like their grandmothers.

'And,' says a strong-minded lady, 'are they any worse companions now for men than they were then?'

'Opinions are various, madam.' I used to write that as a text-hand copy in a nicely-ruled book that I used to blot with inky fingers. You, madam, who claim your rights, surely will not deny me mine—to have my own opinion, which I will dare to give, and say:

'Yes; I think they have not improved. Somehow one likes softness and sweetness in a woman, and your classic young ladies are often very sharp and hard.

'If you combat my opinion upon the main idea of women's purpose here, add this to your study—the aspect of a woman when she is most beautiful.

'And when is that?—in her ball dress?—in her wedding costume?—when she first says "yes?"'

'Oh, no; none of these, but when she is alone with the child she loves, and that sweet—well, angelic look of satisfied maternity is on her face, and there is Nature's own truth stamped indelibly as it has been from the first.

'Men never look like that. They never did, and one may say never will. It is not given to us, madam. Study that look; it is more convincing than all the speeches women ever spoke on woman's rights.'

Just such a look was upon the face of little thin whitefaced Miss Clode, as the frank, manly young fellow strode suddenly into her shop, making her start, change colour, and set down on the counter something she was holding, taking it up again directly with trembling hands.

'Ah, Miss Clode,' he said cheerfully, 'here I am again. Is it the weather, or are your strings bad?'

'Do they break so, then?' she said, hurriedly producing a tin canister, which refused to give up its lid; and Richard had to take it, and wrench it off with his strong fingers, when a number of oily rings of transparent catgut flew out on to the glass case.

'How clumsy I am,' he said.

'No,' she said softly; 'how strong and manly. How you have altered these last ten years!'

'Well, I suppose so,' he said, smiling down at the little

thin, upturned, admiring face. 'But you'll ruin me in strings, Miss Clode.'

'I wish you would not pay for them,' she said plaintively. 'I get the very best Roman strings. I send on purpose to a place in Covent Garden, London, and they ought to be good.'

'And so they are,' he said, taking up half a dozen rings on his fingers and examining them to see which were the clearest, smoothest, and most transparent.

'But they break so,' she sighed. 'You really must not pay for these.'

'Then I shall not have any,' he said.

She gazed tenderly in his face, and her eyes were very intent as she watched him. Then, coughing slightly, and half turning away, she said gently:

'And your father—is he quite well?'

'Oh yes, thank you. Very well. Well as a man can be who has such a great idle, useless son.'

Miss Clode shook her little curls at him reproachfully, and there was something very tender in her way as she cried, 'You should not say that.' Then, in a quiet apologetic manner, she lowered her tone and said:

'You can't help being so tall and strong and manly, and —and—and—I'm only an old woman, Mr. Linnell,' she said, smiling in a deprecating way, 'and I've known you since you were such a boy, so I shall say it—you won't be vain—so handsome.'

'Am I?' he said, laughing. 'Ah well, handsome is that handsome does, Miss Clode.'

'Exactly,' she said, laying her hand upon his arm and speaking very earnestly, 'and I have three—three notes here.'

'For me?' he said, blushing like a woman, and then frowning at his weakness.

'Yes, Mr. Linnell, for you.'

'Tear them up, then,' he said sharply. 'I don't want them.'

Miss Clode gave vent to a sigh of relief.

'Or no,' he said firmly. 'They were given to you to deliver. Give them to me.'

She passed three triangular notes to him half unwillingly, and he took them, glanced at the handwritings, and then tore them across without opening them.

'No lady worth a second thought would address a man like that,' he said sharply. 'Where shall I throw this stuff?'

Miss Clode stooped down and lifted a waste-paper basket from behind the counter, and he threw the scraps in.

'We are old friends, Miss Clode,' he said. 'Burn them for me, please, at once. I should not like to be so dishonourable as to disgrace the writers by letting them be seen.'

'People are talking about you so, sir.'

'About me?' he cried.

'Yes, Mr. Linnell; they say you behaved like a hero.'

' Absurd !'

' When you swam out to the pony carriage and helped to rescue those—er—ladies.'

' My dear Miss Clode, would not any fisherman on the beach have done the same if he had been near? I wish people would not talk such nonsense.'

' People will talk down here, Mr. Linnell. They have so little else to do.'

' More's the pity,' said Richard pettishly.

' And is—is Mrs. Dean quite well again, Mr. Linnell ?'

' Oh yes,' he said coolly. ' She was more frightened than hurt.'

' Does Miss Dean seem any worse, sir ? Does she look pale ?'

The little woman asked these questions in a hesitating way, her hands busy the while over various objects on her counter.

' Pale—pale ?' said Richard, turning over the violin strings and looking to see which were the most clear. ' Really, I did not notice, Miss Clode.'

' He would not speak so coolly if this affair had ripened into anything more warm than being on friendly terms,' thought the little woman, and she seemed to breathe more freely.

' I'm afraid I've been very rude,' continued the young man. ' I ought to have asked after them this morning.'

Miss Clode gave another sigh of relief.

'No one shall see those scraps, Mr. Linnell,' she said quietly; and the look of affectionate pride in him seemed to intensify. 'It is quite right that a young gentleman like you should have some one to love him, but not in such a way as that.'

'No,' he replied shortly, and the colour came into his cheeks again, making them tingle, so that he stamped his foot and snatched up the violin strings again to go on with his selection. 'There, I shall have these four,' he said, forcing a smile, 'and if they don't turn out well I shall patronize your rival, Miss Clode.'

'My rival!' exclaimed the little woman, turning pale. 'Oh, I understand. Yes, of course, Mr. Linnell. Those four. Let me put them in paper.'

'No, no. I'll slip them in this little case,' he said, and he laid four shillings on the counter.

'I'd really much rather you did not pay for them,' she protested, and very earnestly too.

'Then I won't have them,' he said; and, with a sigh, Miss Clode placed the money in her drawer.

'I hope you were not one of the party who serenaded a certain lady on that terrible night of horrors, Mr. Linnell,' she said, smiling; and then, noticing quickly the start he gave, 'Why, fie! I did not think you thought of such things.'

'Yes; don't talk about it, I beg,' he exclaimed. 'It was by accident. I did not know I was going there.'

'But surely, Mr. Linnell, you don't think——Oh!'

She stood gazing at him with her lips apart.

'Miss Clode,' he said firmly, 'I do not confide to people what I think. Good-morning.'

'No, no: stop,' she said earnestly; and he turned, wondering at her tone of voice, and agitation.

'What do you mean?' he said.

'Only—only—that I have known you so long, Mr. Linnell, I can't help—humbly, of course—taking a little interest in you—you made me feel so proud just now—when you tore up those foolish women's letters—and now——'

'Well, and now?' he said sternly.

'It troubled me—pray don't be angry with me—it troubled me—to think—of course it was foolish of me, but I should not—should not like to see you——'

'Well, Miss Clode, pray speak,' for she had stopped again.

'See you make an unworthy choice,' she faltered.

'Miss Clode, this is too much,' he said, flushing angrily, and he turned and left the shop, the little thin pale woman gazing after him wistfully and sighing bitterly as he passed from her sight.

'I'm—I'm very fond of him,' she said as she wiped a few weak tears from her eyes. 'Such a brave, upright, noble young fellow, and so gentle one moment, and so full of spirit the next. Dear, dear, dear, what a thing it is! He never wastes money in gambling, and wine and follies. Perhaps he would though, if he were as rich as the rest of them. And he ought to be.'

She wiped her eyes again, and as she did so the woman's entire aspect changed. For just then Miss Cora Dean was driven by in a hired carriage, her dark eyes flashing, half veiled as they were by the long fringe of lashes, and then she was gone.

'Ah!' exclaimed Miss Clode angrily, 'you are a beauty, sitting up there as haughty as a duchess, and your wicked old mother lying back there in her silks and satins and laces, as if all Saltinville belonged to you, instead of being drowned. But mind this, my fine madams, I may be only little Miss Clode at the library, but if you work any harm between you to those I love I'll have you both bundled neck and crop out of the place, or I'll know the reason why.

'A wretch!' she said, after a pause. 'She'd like nothing better than to tempt him to follow her. But he won't! No; he's thinking of that girl Claire, and she is not half good enough for him. I don't like them and their fine ways. I don't like Denville with his mincing, idiotic airs. How that man can go about as he does with the stain of that poor old woman's death at his house astounds me.

'Well, poor wretch,' she said scornfully, 'it is his trade, as this miserable go-between business is mine. Perhaps he has fallen as low as I have; but I don't live as he does—as if he had thousands a year, when they are next door to starving and horribly in debt.

' Ah, well, it is to make a good show in his shop,' she went on, speaking very bitterly—' to dress the window, and sell his girls, and start his boys.

' Nice bargain he has made in selling one. There's something more about that wretched little empty-headed child than I know, but I shall find out yet. Surely he does not think of that boy and Drelincourt. Oh, it would be too absurd. I've not seen the other brother lately. What a family! And for that boy to be taken with—oh, I must stop it if I can.

' Mrs. Burnett? Yes, I must know about her. There was a great deal going on with that poor young artist who went away—and died. There was some mystery about that, I know, and——'

' What are you talking about, auntie? I thought there was some one in the shop, and came to see if you wanted me.'

' Talking? I talking? Oh, nonsense, my dear. I was only thinking aloud.'

' Well, auntie, it was very loud, for I heard you say you would have to find out something about Mrs. Burnett.'

' You heard me say that? Nonsense!'

' But I did, auntie; and, do you know, I could tell you something so funny about her.'

12—2

'You could, child?' cried the little woman fiercely.

'Yes, and about Mr. Richard Linnell, too.'

Miss Clode caught the girl by the arm, and held her tightly while she seemed to be gasping for breath.

'About May Burnett?——about Richard Linnell?'

'Yes, auntie, for do you know the other night as I was going down by the lower cliff to see if Fisherman Dick had——'

'Hush!' cried Miss Clode, pressing her arm so sharply that the girl winced. 'Here she is.'

CHAPTER XX.

BARCLAY'S TENANTS.

'It was scandalous,' Saltinville said, 'that she should accept it.'

But she did : a handsome little carriage that came down from Long Acre, and was sent round to the stables, where Cora Dean's ponies were put up and kept now on a shorter allowance of corn.

The note was a simple one, written in a very large hand that was decidedly shaky. There was a coronet on the top, and its owner, Lord Carboro', begged Miss Dean's acceptance of the little gift, with his sorrow that he was the cause of the mishap, and his congratulations that she was not hurt.

This was all very refined and in accordance with etiquette. The postscript looked crotchety.

'P.S.—Tell your people not to give them so much corn.'

Cora did so, and said that she should drive out to show the people of Saltinville that she was no coward.

'Then I'll go with you, Betsy,' said Mrs. Dean, ' to show 'em I ain't, too : and, you mark my words, this 'll be the making of you in society.'

So Cora took her drives as of old, found that she was very much noticed by the gentlemen, very little by the ladies, but waited her time.

The Deans lodged at one of the best houses in the Parade —a large, double-fronted place facing the sea, with spacious balcony and open hall door, and porch ornamented with flowers.

The little groom sprang down and ran to the ponies' heads as his mistress alighted, and after sweeping her rich dress aside, held out her hand for her mother, who got out of the carriage slowly, and in what was meant for a very stately style, her quick beady eyes having shown her that the windows on either side of the front door were wide open, while her sharp ears and her nose had already given her notice that the lodgers were at home—a low buzzing mellow hum with a wild refrain in high notes, announcing that old Mr. Linnell was at work with his violoncello to his son's violin, and a faint penetrating perfume—or smell, according to taste—suggesting that Colonel Mellersh was indulging in a cigar.

Mrs. Dean's daughter was quite as quick in detecting these signs, and, raising her head and half closing her eyes, she swept gracefully into the house, unconscious of the fact that Richard Linnell drew back a little from the window on one side of the door, and that Colonel Mellersh showed his teeth as he lay back in his chair beside a small table, on which was a dealt-out pack of cards.

'I should like to poison that old woman,' said the Colonel, gathering together the cards.

'I wish Mr. Barclay had let the first floor to some one else, Richard,' said a low pleasant voice from the back of the room. *P-r-r-rm, Pr-um!*

The speaker did not say *Pr-r-rm, Pr-um!* That sound was produced by an up and down draw of the bow across the fourth string of the old violoncello he held between his legs, letting the neck of the instrument with its pegs fall directly after into the hollow of his arm, as he picked up a cake of amber-hued transparent rosin from the edge of a music stand, and began thoughtfully to rub it up and down the horse-hair of the bow.

The speaker's was a pleasant handsome face of a man approaching sixty; but though his hair was very grey, he was remarkably well preserved. His well-cut rather effeminate face showed but few lines, and there was just a tinge of colour in his cheeks, such as good port wine might have produced: but in this case it was a consequence of a calm, peaceful, seaside life. He was evidently slight and tall, but bent, and in his blue eyes there was a dreamy look, while a curious twitch came over his face from time to time as if he suffered pain.

'It would have been better, father,' said Richard Linnell, turning over the leaves of a music-book with his violin bow, 'but we can't pick and choose whom one is to sit next in this world.'

'No, no, we can't, my son.'

'And I don't think that we ought to trouble ourselves about our neighbours, so long as they behave themselves decorously here.'

'No, no, my son,' said Linnell, senior, thoughtfully. 'There's a deal of wickedness in this world, but I suppose we mustn't go about throwing stones.'

'I'm not going to, father, and I'm sure you wouldn't throw one at a mad dog.'

'Don't you think I would, Dick?' with a very sweet smile ; and the eyes brightened and looked pleased. 'Well, perhaps you are right.   Poor brute !   Why should I add to its agony ?'

'So long as it didn't bite, eh, father ?'

'To be sure, Dick ; so long as it didn't bite.   I should like to run through that *adagio* again, Dick, but not if you're tired, my boy, not if you're tired.'

'Tired ?   No !' cried the young man.   'I could keep on all day.'

'That's right.   I'm glad I taught you.   There's something so soul-refreshing in a bit of music, especially when you are low-spirited.'

'Which you never are, now.'

'N—no, not often, say not often, say not often. It makes me a little low-spirited though about that woman and her mother, Dick.'

'I don't see why it should.'

'But it does. Such a noble-looking beautiful creature, and such a hard, vulgar, worldly mother. Ah, Dick, beautiful women are to be pitied.'

'No, no : to be admired,' said Richard, laughing.

'Pitied, my boy, pitied,' said the elder, making curves in the air with his bow, while the fingers of his left hand— long, thin, white, delicate fingers—stopped the strings, as if he were playing the bars of some composition. 'Your plain women scout their beautiful sisters, and trample upon them, but it is in ignorance. They don't know the temptations that assail one who is born to good looks.'

'Why, father, this is quite a homily.'

'Ah, yes, Dick,' he said, laughing. 'I ought to have been a preacher, I think, I am always prosing. Poor things— poor things ! A lovely face is often a curse.'

'Oh, don't say that.'

'But I do say it, Dick. It is a curse to that woman upstairs. Never marry a beautiful woman, Dick.'

'But you did, father.'

The old man started violently and changed colour, but recovered himself on the instant.

' Yes, yes. She was very beautiful. And she died, Dick ; she died.'

He bent his head over his music, and Richard crossed and laid his hand upon his shoulder.

' I am sorry I spoke so thoughtlessly.'

' Oh, no, my boy ; oh, no. It was quite right. She was a very beautiful woman. That miniature does not do her justice. But—but don't marry a beautiful woman, Dick,' he continued, gazing wistfully into his son's face. ' Now that *adagio*. It is a favourite bit of mine.'

Richard Linnell looked as if he would have liked to speak, and there was a troubled expression on his face as he thought of Claire Denville's sweet candid eyes ; but he shrank from any avowal. For how dare he, when she had given him but little thought, and—well, she was a beautiful woman, one of those against whom he had been warned.

He looked up and found his father watching him keenly, when both assumed ignorance of any other matter than the *adagio* movement, the sweet notes of which, produced by the thrilling strings, floated out through the open window, and up and in that of the drawing-room floor overhead, where on a luxurious couch Mrs. Dean had thrown herself, while her daughter was slowly pacing the room with the air of a tragedy queen.

' Buzz-buzz ; boom-boom ! Oh, those horrid fiddlers !' cried Mrs. Dean, bouncing up and crossing to the fireplace, where she caught up the poker; but only to have her hand seized by her daughter, who took the poker away, and replaced it in the fender.

'What are you going to do?'

'What am I going to do? Why thump on the floor to make them quiet. Do you suppose I'm going to sit here and be driven mad with their scraping! This isn't a play house!'

'You will do nothing of the sort, mother.'

'Oh, won't I? Do you think I'm going to pay old Barclay all that money for these rooms, and not have any peace? Pray who are you talking to?'

'To you, mother,' said Cora sternly; and the stoutly-built, brazen-looking virago shrank from her daughter's fierce gaze. 'You must not forget yourself here, among all these respectable people.'

'And pray who's going to? But I don't know so much about your respectability. That Colonel, with his queer looks like the devil in "Dr. Faustus," is no better than he should be.'

'The Colonel is a man of the world like the rest,' said Cora coldly.

'Yes, and a nice man of the world, too. And that old Linnell's living apart from his wife. I know though——'

'Silence!'

'Now look here, Betsy, I won't have you say *silence* to

me like that. This here isn't the stage, and we aren't
playing parts. Just you speak to me proper, madam.'

'Mother, I will not have you speak of Mr. Linnell like that.'

'Ho, indeed! And why not, pray? Now, look here,
Betsy,' she cried, holding up a warning finger, 'I won't
have no nonsense there. I'm not a fool. I know the
world. I've seen you sighing and looking soft when we've
passed that young fellow downstairs.'

Cora's eyes seemed to burn as she fixedly returned her
mother's look.

'Oh, you may stare, madam; but I can see more than
you think Why, you ought to be ashamed of yourself,
making eyes at a poor, penniless fiddler, when you might——'

'I—I don't want to quarrel, mother,' cried Cora, 'but if
you dare to speak to me again like that I'll not be answerable
for myself.'

'There!—there!—there! There's gratitude!'

'Gratitude? Where should I have been but for Mr.
Linnell's bravery, and which of the wretched dressed-up
and titled dandies stirred to save me the other day? Richard
Linnell is a brave, true-hearted man, too good to marry an
actress.'

'She's mad—she's mad—she's mad! There's grace;
and to her mother, too, who's thought of nothing but getting
her on in the world, and brought her forward, so that now
she can live on the best of everything, in the handsomest of

rooms, and keep her carriage. She flies in her poor mother's face, and wants to get rid of her, I suppose. Oho—oho—oh!'

Mrs. Dean plumped herself down into a gilded chair, and began to howl very softly.

'Don't be a fool, mother,' said Cora. 'I don't want to quarrel, I tell you, so hold your tongue.'

'After the way I've brought her up, too,' howled Mrs. Dean—softly, so that the sound should not be heard downstairs.

'After the way you've brought me up!' cried Cora fiercely. 'Yes; brought me up to be sneered at by every lady I meet —brought me up so that I hate myself, and long sometimes to be one of the poor women we see knitting stockings on the beach.'

'Don't be a fool, Cory, my handsome, beautiful gal,' cried Mrs. Dean, suddenly starting up in her seat, dry-eyed and forgetful of her grief. 'How can you be so stupid!'

'Stupid!' cried Cora bitterly. 'Is it stupid to wish myself a woman that some true-hearted man could love, instead of looking forward to a life of acting.'

'Oh, how you do go on to be sure. I am surprised at you, Cory. I know what you'd say about the life as them leads as ar'n't in the profession, but don't you be a fool, Betsy. "Your face is your fortune, sir, she said," as the song says; working your fingers to the bone won't keep you out of the workus. Don't tell me. I know. I've known them as has tried it. Let them work as likes. I like a cutlet and a glass of fine sherry, and some well-made coffee with a noo-laid egg in it, and it ain't to be got by folks as works their fingers to the bone.'

' And who wants to work their fingers to the bone, mother?' cried Cora, tearing off and flinging down her handsome feathered hat. ' In every face I see there's the look— " You're only one of the stage-players—a rogue and a vagabond." I want to lead some life for which I need not blush.'

' As she needn't blush for! Oh, dear, oh, dear! When her father trod the boards and her mother was born on 'em ! What a gal you are, Betsy,' said Mrs. Dean, who professed high good humour now, and she rocked herself to and fro, and pressed her hands on her knees as she laughed. ' Oh, I say, Cory, you are a one. You will act the injured fine lady in private life, my dear. Why, what a silly thing you are. Look at that hat you've chucked down. Didn't it cost five guineas ?'

' Yes, mother, it cost five guineas,' said Cora wearily.

' And you can have whatever you like. Oh, I say, my lovely gal, for you really are, you know, don't get into these silly fits. It's such stuff. Why, who knows what may happen ? You may be right up atop of the tree yet, and how about yon folks as passes you by now ? Why, they'll all be as civil and friendly as can be. There, there, come

and kiss me, ducky, we musn't quarrel, must we? I've got
my eyes open for you, so don't, don't, there's a dear. I
know what these things means—don't go chucking yourself
at that young Linnell's head.'

'Let Mr. Linnell alone, mother.'

'But I can't, my luvvy; I know too well what these
things mean. Why, there was Julia Jennings as was at the
Lane—it was just afore you was born. There was a dook
and a couple of lords, and carridges and horses, and livery
suvvants, and as many jewels and dymonds and dresses as
she liked to order; and if she didn't kick 'em all over and
marry a shopman, and lived poor ever after. Now do, my
luvvy, be advised by me. I know what the world is, and——
Gracious goodness! there's somebody coming up the
stairs.'

Mrs. Dean threw herself into an attitude meant to be easy,
and Cora smoothed her knitted brows as there was a knock
at the door, and, after a loud 'Come in,' a neat-looking
maid entered.

'Mr. Barclay, please, ma'am.'

'Show him up, Jane,' said Mrs. Dean sharply; and then,
as the door closed, 'The old rip's come after his rent. How
precious sharp he is.'

'Morning, ladies,' said Barclay. 'I heard you were in.
Glad to see you are no worse for your accident the other
day.'

He glanced at Cora, who bowed rather stiffly, and said 'Not at all.'

'I can't say that, Mr. Barclay. I'm a bit shook; but, as I said to my daughter, I wasn't going to show the white feather, and the ponies go lovely now.'

'Well, I'm glad of that.'

'And I'm so much obliged to you for helping of me. Do you know, it was just like a scene in a piece we—er—saw once at the Lane.'

'Oh, it was nothing ma'am, what I did. Miss Dean, there, she took off all the honours. No cold, I hope.'

Cora did not answer.

'Plucky fellow, young Linnell; but poor, you know, poor.'

'So I've heard,' said Mrs. Dean maliciously. 'I was thinking of sending him ten guineas.'

'Oh, I wouldn't do that, ma'am,' said Barclay.

'Oh, well, I must say *thankye* some other way. Very kind of you to call. I said to my daughter, "There's Mr. Barclay come for his rent," but I was wrong.'

'Not you, ma'am,' said Barclay, whose eyes were rapidly taking in the state of the room. 'Business is business, you know,' and he took another glance at the rich furniture and handsome mirrors of the place.

'Oh, it's all right, Mr. Barclay. We're taking the greatest care of it all, and your rent's all ready for you, and always will be, of course.'

' Yes, yes, I know that, ma'am. I've brought you a little receipt. Saves trouble. Pen and ink not always ready. I keep to my days. So much pleasanter for everybody. Nice rooms, ain't they?' he added, turning to Cora.

' Yes, Mr. Barclay, the rooms are very nice,' she said coldly and thoughtfully.

' Anything the matter with her?' said Mr. Barclay, leaning forward to Mrs. Dean, and taking the money she handed in exchange for a receipt. ' Not in love, is she?'

Mrs. Dean and her visitor exchanged glances, and smiled as Cora rose and walked to the window to gaze out at the sea, merely turning her head to bow distantly when the landlord rose to leave.

' I'm a regular scoundrel, 'pon my soul I am,' said Josiah Barclay, rubbing his nose with the edge of a memorandum book; 'but they pay very handsomely, and if I were to refuse to let a part of a house that I furnish on purpose for letting, without having the highest moral certificates of character with the people who want the rooms, I'm afraid I should never let them at all. Bah! it's no business of mine.'

He went back to the front door and knocked, to be shown in directly after to where Colonel Mellersh was sitting back in his chair, having evidently just thrown down the pack of cards.

' Morning, Shylock,' he said, showing his white teeth. ' Want your pound of flesh again?'

'No, thank ye, Colonel; rather have the ducats. I say, though, I wish you wouldn't call me Shylock. I'm not one of the chosen, you know.'

'That I'll take oath you're not, Barclay,' said the Colonel, looking at his visitor with a very amused smile. 'Your future is thoroughly assured. I'm sorry for you, Barclay, for I don't think you're the worst scoundrel that ever breathed.'

'I say, you know, Colonel, this is too bad, you know. Come, come, come.'

'Oh, I always speak plainly to you, Barclay. Let me see; can you let me have a hundred?'

'A hundred, Colonel?' said the other, looking up sharply; 'well, yes, I think I can.'

'Ah, well, I don't want it, Barclay. I know you'd be only too glad to get a good hold of me.'

'Wrong, Colonel, wrong,' said Barclay, chuckling as he glanced at the cards. 'You do me too much good for that.'

'Do I?' said the Colonel, smiling in a peculiarly cynical way. 'Well, perhaps I do influence your market a little. There,' he said, taking some notes from his little pocket-book, and handing them to his visitor, 'now we are free once more.'

'Thankye, Colonel, thankye. You're a capital tenant. I say, by the way, after all these years, I shouldn't like to do anything to annoy you: I hope you don't mind the actors upstairs.'

' No,' said the Colonel, staring at him.

' Because if you did complain, and were not satisfied, I'd make a change, you know.'

' Don't trouble the women for my sake,' said the Colonel gruffly. ' Look here, Barclay, how would you play this hand ?'

He took up the cards as he spoke, shuffled them with an easy, graceful movement, the pieces of pasteboard flying rapidly through his hands, before dealing them lightly out upon the table, face upwards, and selecting four thirteens.

' Now,' he said, ' look here. Your partner holds two trumps—six, nine ; your adversaries right and left have knave and ace ; B. on your right leads trumps—what would you do ?'

Barclay knit his brow and took the Colonel's hand, gazing from one to the other thoughtfully, and then, without a word, played the hand, the Colonel selecting those cards that would be played by the others till the hand was half through, when Barclay hesitated for a moment, and then seemed to throw away a trick.

' Why did you do that ?' said the Colonel sharply.

' Because by losing that I should get the next two.'

' Exactly !' cried the Colonel with his eyes flashing. ' That endorses my opinion. Barclay, I shan't play against you if

13—2

I can help myself. Money-lending seems to sharpen the wits wonderfully. What a clever old fox you are!'

'One's obliged to be clever now a days, Colonel, if one wants to get on. Well, I must go. I have to see your neighbours. Rents are very bad to get in.'

' I suppose so,' said the Colonel drily. ' Good-morning.'

' I wonder what he makes a year by his play,' said Barclay to himself, as he went back to the front door to knock for the third time. ' I believe he plays square, too, but he has a wonderful head, and he's practising night and day. Now for old Linnell.'

He was shown into Mr. Linnell's room the next minute, to find that he was expected, and that he was gravely and courteously received, and his rent paid, so that there was nothing for him to do but say ' Good-morning.' But Josiah Barclay's conscience was a little uneasy, and in spite of the fact that his tenant was far from being a rich man, there was something in his grave refined manner that won his respect.

' Wish you'd come and see us sometimes, Mr. Linnell, just in a friendly way, you know. Chop and glass o' sherry with Mrs. Barclay and me; and you'd join us too, Mr. Richard, eh ?'

' Thank you, Mr. Barclay, no,' said Richard's father; ' I never go out. Richard, my son, here, would, I dare say, accept your invitation.'

'Oh, but can't you too, eh? Look here, you know, you're a man who loves bits of old china, and I've quite a lot. Really good. Come: when shall it be?'

'Don't press me now, Mr. Barclay,' said his tenant gravely. 'Perhaps some other time.'

'Then you're offended, Mr. Linnell. You're a bit hipped because of the other lodgers, you know.'

'Mr. Barclay, I have made no complaints,' said the elder Linnell quietly.

'No, you've made no complaints, but you show it in your way, don't you see. It wasn't for me to be too strict in my inquiries about people, Mr. Linnell. I'm sorry I offended you; but what can I do?'

'Mr. Barclay has a perfect right to do what he pleases with his own house,' replied the elder Linnell with dignity. 'Good-day.'

'Now I could buy that man up a hundred times over,' grumbled Barclay as he walked away, richer by many pounds than when he started on his journey that morning; 'but he always seems to set me down; to look upon me with contempt; and young Richard is as high and mighty as can be. Ah, well, wait a bit!—"Can you oblige me with fifty pounds, Mr. Barclay, on my note of hand?"—and then p'raps they'll be more civil.

'Things ain't pleasant though, just now. One house made notorious by a murder, and me letting a couple of actresses lodge in another. Well, they pay regular, and I dare say she'll make a good match somewhere before long ; but I'm afraid, when the old lady gets to know they're stage people, there'll be a bit of a breeze.'

CHAPTER XXI.

DICK CATCHES—SHRIMPS.

THERE was quite a little crowd at the end of the pier to see Fisherman Dick and some others busy with boathooks searching for the fragments of Cora Dean's pony carriage, and for want of something better to stare at, the fastening of a rope to first one pair of wheels and then to the other, and the hauling ashore, formed thrilling incidents.

Two rich carriage-cloaks were cast ashore by the tide, miles away, and the rug was found right under the pier, but there were several articles still missing. Cora's reticule, containing her purse and cut-glass scent-bottle; a little carriage-clock used by Mrs. Dean, who was always very particular about the lapse of time, and that lady's reticule and purse.

It was Fisherman Dick's special task to search for them when the tide was low, and this he did by going to work as a setter does in a field, quartering the ground and hunting it all over to and fro.

But Fisherman Dick did his work with a shrimping net, and one day he took home the little carriage-clock and showed it to his wife.

Another day he found Mrs. Dean's reticule, and caught a great many shrimps as well.

Then the tide did not serve for several days, and he had to wait, shaking his head and telling Mrs. Miggles he was afraid the sand would have covered everything.

'' Then give it up,' said Mrs. Miggles, who was trying to sew with the little girl in her lap, but was prevented by the tiny thing making dashes at her broad-brimmed silver spectacles, which it kept taking off and flourishing in one little plump hand.

' Well done, little 'un,' cried the fisherman, grinning. ' No, missus, I don't like being beat.'

He went off, looking very serious, with his net over one shoulder, the creel over the other, and after going to and fro patiently waist and often breast deep, he was successful in finding Cora Dean's reticule, with its purse and cut-glass bottle ; and that night he went home amply rewarded, Cora having been very generous, and Mrs. Dean saying several times over that she wouldn't have believed that a great rough man like that would have been so honest.

' I declare, Betsy, he's just like a man in a play—the good man who finds the treasure and gives it up.   Why, he might

have kep' your puss, and my puss too, and nobody been a
bit the wiser.'

That was all that was missing; but every day for a week,
during the times that the tide was low, Fisherman Dick was
busy, pushing his shrimping-net before him, and stopping
every now and then to raise it, throw out the rubbish, and
transfer the few shrimps he caught to his creel.

It was not a good place for shrimping—it was too deep;
but he kept on with his laborious task, wading out as far as
ever he could go; and more than one of his fellow-mermen
grinned at his empty creel.

' Why don't you try the shallows, Dick?' said one of the
blue-jerseyed fellows, who seemed to be trying to grow a
hump on his back by leaning over the rail at the edge of the
cliff.

' 'Cause I like to try the deeps,' growled Fisherman Dick.

' Ah, you want to make your fortune too quick, my lad;
that's plain.'

Dick winked, and went home; and the next day he
winked, and went out shrimping again, and caught very
few, and went home again, put on his dry clothes, and said:

' Give us the babby.'

Mrs. Miggles gave him the ' babby,' and Dick took her
and nursed her, smiling down at the little thing as she
climbed up his chest, and tangled her little fingers in his
great beard; while Mrs. Miggles gave the few shrimps a

pick over and a shake up before she consigned the hopping unfortunates to the boiling bath that should turn them from blackish grey to red.

' What is it, old man ?' said Mrs. Miggles ; ' sperrits ?'

Fisherman Dick shook his head, and began to sing gruffly to the child about a ' galliant ' maiden who went to sea in search of her true ' lovy-er along of a British crew.'

' What is it, then—lace ?'

Fisherman Dick shook his head again, and bellowed out the word ' crew,' the little child looking at him wonderingly, but not in the least alarmed.

' I never did see such an oyster as you are, old man,' said Mrs. Miggles.   ' You're the closest chap in the place.'

' Ay !' said Fisherman Dick; and he went on with his song.

He went shrimping off the end of the pier for the delecta-tion of the mincing crowd of promenaders twice more.   Lord Carboro' saw him ; so did Major Rockley and Sir Harry Payne.   Sir Matthew Bray was too busy dancing attendance upon Lady Drelincourt to pay any attention.

The Master of the Ceremonies saw him too, as he bowed to one, smiled upon a second, and took snuff with a third ; and several times, as he watched the fisherman wading out there, he followed his movements attentively, and appeared to be gazing without his mask of artificiality.

The man's calm, dreamy ways seemed to have an attraction, as if he were wishing that he could change places with him, and lead so simple and peaceful a life. And as he watched him, very far out now, Dick raised his net, emptied it, shook it with his back to the people, and then began to wade in quite another direction, going back no more to the ground off the pier.

The Master of the Ceremonies did not look himself that day, and twice over he found himself on the edge of the pier gazing out to sea, where everything seemed so peaceful and still.

There was a buzz of voices going on about him, but he heard nothing, till all at once a voice, quite familiar to him, exclaimed sharply :

' Well, what is it ?'

' Message from Mr. Barclay, sir.'

' Well ?'

' I took your note, sir, and he'll be glad to see you to-morrow morning at twelve.'

' That will do.   Now take the other.'

Stuart Denville could not restrain himself as he heard those voices just behind, and it was as if some power had turned him sharply round to see Major Rockley in conversation with one of the private dragoons of his regiment.

The man had delivered his message to his master, and then turned stiffly to go, coming face to face with Denville, whose whole manner changed.   He turned deadly pale, of an unwholesome pallor, and then the blood seemed to flush to his face and head. His eyes flashed and his lips parted as if to speak, but the dragoon saluted, turned upon his heel, and strode away.

'Anything the matter, Denville?' said the Major, who had seen something of the encounter.

'Matter, matter,' said the old man hoarsely, and he now began to tremble violently. 'No—no,—a little faint. You'll pardon me,—a chair,—a——'

The old man would have fallen, but the Major caught his arm and helped him to a seat, where a crowd of fashionables surrounded him, and did all they possibly could to prevent his recovery from his fit by keeping away every breath of air, and thrusting at him bottles of salts, vinaigrettes, and scents of every fashionable kind.

'What's the matter with the old fellow?' said the Major, as he twirled his moustache. 'Could he have known about the note? Impossible; and if he had known, why should he turn faint? Bah! Absurd! The heat. He's little better than a shadow, after all.'

CHAPTER XXII.

A SURREPTITIOUS VISITOR.

'Major Rockley's servant to see you, miss.'

Claire started from her seat and looked at Footman Isaac with a troubled expression that was full of shame and dread.

She dropped her eyes on the instant as she thought of her position.

It was four o'clock, and the promenade on cliff and pier in full swing. Her father would not be back for two hours, Morton was away somewhere, and it was so dreadful—so degrading—to be obliged to see her brother, the prodigal, in the servants' part of the house.

For herself she would not have cared, but it was lowering her brother; and, trying to be calm and firm, she said:

'Show him in here, Isaac.'

'In here, miss?'

'Yes.'

'Please ma'am, master said——'

'Show him in here, Isaac,' said Claire, drawing herself

up with her eyes flashing, and the colour returning to her
cheeks.

The footman backed out quickly, and directly after there
was the clink of spurs, and a heavy tread.   Then the door
opened and closed, and Major Rockley's servant, James
Bell, otherwise Fred Denville, strode into the room; and
Isaac's retreating steps were heard.

'Fred!' cried Claire, throwing her arms round his neck,
and kissing the handsome bronzed face again and again.

'My darling girl!' he cried, holding her tightly to his
breast, while his face lit up as he returned her caresses.

'Oh, Fred!' she said, as she laid her hands then upon
his shoulders and gazed at him at arm's length, 'you've
been drinking.'

'One half-pint of ale.   That's all: upon my soul,' he said.
'I say, I wish it were not wicked to commit murder.'

If he had by some blow paralyzed her he could not have
produced a greater change in her aspect, for her eyes grew
wild and the colour faded out of her cheeks and lips.

'Don't look like that,' he said, smiling. 'I shan't do it—
at least, not while I'm sober; but I should like to wring that
supercilious scoundrel's neck.   He looks down upon me in
a way that is quite comical.'

'Why did you come, dear?' said Claire sadly.   'Oh, Fred,
if I could but buy you out, so that you could begin life
again.'

'No good, my dear little girl,' he said tenderly. 'There's something wrong in my works. I've no stability, and I should only go wrong again.'

'But, if you would try, Fred.'

'Try, my pet!' he said fiercely; 'Heaven knows how I did try, but the drink was too much for me. If we had been brought up to some honest way of making a living, and away from this sham, I might have been different, but it drove me to drink, and I never had any self-command. I'm best where I am; obliged to be sober as the Major's servant.'

There was a contemptuous look in his eyes as he said this last.

'And that makes it so much worse,' sighed Claire with a sad smile. 'If you were only the King's servant—a soldier —I would not so much mind.'

'Perhaps it is best as it is,' he said sternly.

'Don't say that, Fred dear.'

'But I do say it, girl. If I had been brought up differently —Bah! I didn't come here to grumble about the old man.'

'No, no, pray, pray don't. And, Fred dear, you must not stop. Do you want a little money?'

'Yes!' he cried eagerly. 'No! Curse it all, girl, I wish you would not tempt me. So you are not glad to see me?'

'Indeed, yes, Fred; but you must not stay. If our father were to return there would be such a scene.'

'He will not. He is on the pier, and won't be back these two hours. Where's Morton?'

'Out, dear.'

'Then we are all right. Did you expect me?'

'No, dear. Let me make you some tea.'

'No; stop here. Didn't you expect this?'

He drew a note from his breast.

'That note? No, dear. Who is it from?'

Fred Denville looked his sister searchingly in the face, and its innocent candid expression satisfied him, and he drew a sigh full of relief.

'If it had been May who looked at me like that, I should have said she was telling me a lie.'

'Oh, Fred!'

'Bah! You know it's true. Little wax-doll imp. But I believe you, Claire. Fate's playing us strange tricks. I am James Bell, Major Rockley's servant, and he trusts me with his commissions. This is a *billet-doux*—a love-letter—to my sister, which my master sends, and I am to wait for an answer.'

Claire drew herself up, and as her brother saw the blood mantle in her face, and the haughty, angry look in her eyes as she took the letter and tore it to pieces, he, too, drew himself up, and there was a proud air in his aspect.

'There is no answer to Major Rockley's letter,' she said coldly. 'How dare he write to me!'

'Claire, old girl, I must hug you,' cried the dragoon. 'By George! I feel as if I were not ashamed of the name of Denville after all. I was going to bully you and tell you that my superior officer is as big a scoundrel as ever breathed, and that if you carried on with him I'd shoot you. Now, bully me, my pet, and tell your prodigal drunken dragoon of a brother that he ought to be ashamed of himself for even thinking such a thing. I won't shrink.'

'My dear brother,' she said tenderly, as she placed her hands in his.

'My dear sister,' he said softly, as he kissed her little white hands in turn, 'I need not warn and try to teach you, for I feel that I might come to you for help if I could learn. There—there. Some day you'll marry some good fellow.'

She shook her head.

'Yes, you will,' he said. 'Richard Linnell, perhaps. Don't let the old man worry you into such a match as May's.'

'I shall never marry,' said Claire, in a low strange voice; 'never.'

'Yes, you will,' he said, smiling; 'but what you have to guard against is not the gallantries of the contemptible puppies who haunt this place, but some big match that—— Ah! Too late!'

He caught a glimpse of his father's figure passing the

window, and made for the door, but it was only to stand face to face with the old man, who came in hastily, haggard, and wild of eye.

Fred Denville drew back into the room as his father staggered in, and then, as the door swung to and fastened itself, there was a terrible silence, and Claire looked on speechless for the moment, as she saw her brother draw himself up, military fashion, while her father's face changed in a way that was horrible to behold.

He looked ten years older. His eyes started; his jaw fell, and his hands trembled as he raised them, with the thick cane hanging from one wrist.

He tried to speak, but the words would not come for a few moments.

At last his speech seemed to return, and, in a voice full of rage, hate, and horror combined, he cried furiously:

' You here !—fiend !—wretch !—villain !'

' Oh, father !' cried Claire, darting to his side.

' Hush, Claire ! Let him speak,' said Fred.

' Was it not enough that I forbade you the house before; but, now—to come—to dare—villain !—wretch !—cold-blooded, miserable wretch ! You are no son of mine. Out of my sight ! Curse you ! I curse you with all the bitterness that——'

' Father ! father !' cried Claire, in horrified tones, as she threw herself between them; but, in his rage, the old man struck her across the face with his arm, sending her tottering back.

'Oh, this is too much,' cried Fred, dropping his stolid manner. 'You cowardly——'

'Cowardly! Ha! ha! ha! Cowardly!' screamed the old man, catching at his stick. 'You say that—you?'

As Fred strode towards him, the old man struck him with his cane, a sharp well-directed blow across the left ear, and, stung to madness by the pain, the tall strong man caught the frail-looking old beau by the throat and bore him back into a chair, holding him with one hand while his other was clenched and raised to strike.

CHAPTER XXIII.

FATHER AND DAUGHTER.

'STRIKE! Kill me! Add parricide to your other crimes, dog, and set me free of this weary life,' cried the old man wildly, as he glared in the fierce, distorted face of the sturdy soldier who held him back.

But it wanted not Claire's hand upon Fred Denville's arm to stay the blow. The passionate rage fled as swiftly as it had flashed up, and he tore himself away.

'You shouldn't have struck me,' he cried in a voice full of anguish. 'I couldn't master myself. You struck her—the best and truest girl who ever breathed; and I'd rather be what I am—scamp, drunkard, common soldier, and have struck you down, than you, who gave that poor girl a cowardly blow. Claire—my girl—God bless you! I can come here no more.'

He caught her wildly in his arms, kissed her passionately, and then literally staggered out of the house, and they saw him reel by the window.

There was again a terrible silence in that room, where the old man, looking feeble and strange now, lay back in the chair where he had been thrown, staring wildly straight before him as Claire sank upon the carpet, burying her face in her hands and sobbing to herself.

' And this is home! And this is home!'

She tried to restrain her tears, but they burst forth with sobs more wild and uncontrolled; and at last they had their effect upon the old man, whose wild stare passed off, and, rising painfully in his seat, he glared at the door and shuddered.

' How dare he come!' he muttered. ' How dare he touch her! How——'

He stopped as he turned his eyes upon where Claire crouched, as if he had suddenly become aware of her presence, and his face softened into a piteous yearning look as he stretched out his hands towards her, and then slowly rose to his feet.

' I struck her,' he muttered, ' I struck her. My child— my darling! I—I—Claire—Claire——'

His voice was very low as he slowly sank upon his knees, and softly laid one hand upon her dress, raising it to his lips and kissing it with a curiously strange abasement in his manner.

Claire did not move nor seem to hear him, and he crept nearer to her and timidly laid his hand upon her head.

He snatched it away directly, and knelt there gazing at her wildly, for she shuddered, shrank from him, and, starting to her feet, backed towards the door with such a look of repulsion in her face that the old man clasped his hands together, and his lips parted as if to cry to her for mercy.

But no sound left them, and for a full minute they remained gazing the one at the other. Then, with a heart-rending sob, Claire drew open the door and hurried from the room.

'What shall I do? What shall I do?' groaned Denville as he rose heavily to his feet. 'It is too hard to bear. Better sleep—at once and for ever.'

He sank into his chair with his hands clasped and his elbows resting upon his knees, and he bent lower and lower, as if borne down by the weight of his sorrow; and thus he remained as the minutes glided by, till, hearing a step at last, and the jingle of glass, he rose quickly, smoothed his care-marked face, and thrusting his hand into his breast, began to pace the room, catching up hat and stick, and half closing his eyes, as if in deep thought.

It was a good bit of acting, for when Isaac entered with a tray to lay the dinner cloth, and glanced quickly at his master, it was to see him calm and apparently buried in some plan, with not the slightest trace of domestic care upon his well-masked face.

' Mr. Morton at home, Isaac?' he said, with a slightly affected drawl.

' No, sir; been out hours.'

' Not gone fishing, Isaac?'

' No, sir; I think Mr. Morton's gone up to the barracks, sir. Said he should be back to dinner, sir.'

' That is right, Isaac. That is right. I think I will go for a little promenade before dinner myself.'

' He's a rum un,' muttered the footman as he stood behind the curtain on one side of the window; ' anyone would think we were all as happy as the day's long here, when all the time the place is chock full of horrors, and if I was to speak——'

Isaac did not finish his sentence, but remained watching the Master of the Ceremonies with his careful mincing step till he was out of sight, when the footman turned from the window to stand tapping the dining-table with his finger tips.

' If I was to go, there'd be a regular wreck, and I shouldn't get a penny of my back wages. If I stay, he may get them two well married, and then there'd be money in the house. Better stay. Lor', if people only knew all I could tell 'em about this house, and the scraping, and putting off bills, and the troubles with Miss May and the two boys, and——'

Isaac drew a long breath and turned rather white.

' I feel sometimes as if I ought to make a clean breast of

it, but I don't like to. He isn't such a bad sort, when you come to know him, but that——ugh !'

He shuddered, and began to rattle the knives and forks upon the table, giving one a rub now and then on his shabby livery.

' It's a puzzler,' he said, stopping short, after breathing in a glass, and giving it a rub with a cloth. ' Some day, I suppose, there'll be a difference, and he'll be flush of money. I suppose he daren't start yet. Suppose I—— No ; that wouldn't do. He'll pay all the back, then, and I might——'

Isaac shuddered again, and muttered to himself in a very mysterious way. Then, all at once :

' Why, I might cry halves, and make him set me up for life. Why not ? She was good as gone, and——'

He set down the glass, and wiped the dew that had gathered off his brow, looking whiter than before, for just then a memory had come into Isaac's mental vision—it was a horrible recollection of having been tempted to go and see the execution of a murderer at the county town, and this man's accomplice was executed a month later.

' Accomplice' was an ugly word that seemed to force itself into Isaac's mind, and he shook his head and hurriedly finished laying the cloth.

' Let him pay me my wages, all back arrears,' he said. ' Perhaps there is a way of selling a secret without being an accomplice, but I don't know, and——oh, I couldn't do it. It would kill that poor girl, who's about worried to death with the dreadful business, without there being anything else.'

CHAPTER XXIV.

As a rule, a tailor is one who will give unlimited credit so
long as his client is a man of society, with expectations, and
the maker of garments can charge his own prices; but Stuart
Denville, Esq., M.C., of Saltinville, paid a visit to his tailor
to find that gentleman inexorable.

'No, Mr. Denville, sir, it ain't to be done. I should be
glad to fit out the young man, as he should be fitted out as
a gentleman, sir; but there is bounds to everything.'

'Exactly, my dear Mr. Ping, but I can assure you that
before long both his and my accounts shall be paid.'

'No, sir, can't do it. I'm very busy, too. Why not try
Crowder and Son?'

'My dee—ar Mr. Ping—you'll pardon me? I ask you
as a man, as an artist in your profession, could I see my son
—my heir—a gentleman who I hope some day will make
a brilliant match—a young man who is going at once into
the best of society—could I now, Mr. Ping, see that youth

in a suit of clothes made by Crowder and Son ? Refuse my appeal, if you please, my dear sir, but—you'll pardon me— do not add insult to the injury.'

Mr. Ping was mollified, and rubbed his hands softly. This was flattering : for Crowder and Son, according to his view of the case, did not deserve to be called tailors—certainly not gentlemen's tailors ; but he remained firm.

' No, Mr. Denville, sir, far be it from me to wish to insult you, sir, and I thank you for the amount of custom you've brought me. You can't say as I'm unfair.'

' You'll pardon me, Mr. Ping ; I never did.'

' Thank you, sir; but as I was a saying, you've had clothes of me, sir, for years, and you haven't paid me, sir, and I haven't grumbled, seeing as you've introduced me clients, but I can't start an account for Mr. Denville, junior, sir, and I won't.'

The M.C. took snuff, and rested first on one leg and then on the other ; lastly, he held his head on one side and ad- mired two or three velvet waistcoat pieces, so as to give Mr. Ping time to repent. But Mr. Ping did not want time to repent, and he would not have repented had the M.C. stayed an hour, and this the latter knew, but dared not resent, bowing himself out at last gracefully.

' Good-morning, Mr. Ping, good-morning. I am sorry you —er—but no matter. Lovely day, is it not ?'

' Lovely, sir. Good-morning—poor, penniless, proud,

stuck-up, half-starved old dandy,' muttered the prosperous tradesman, as he stood in his shirt-sleeves at the door, his grey hair all brushed forward into a fierce frise, and a yellow inch tape round his neck like an alderman's chain. 'I wouldn't trust his boy a sixpence to save his life. Prospects, indeed. Fashion, indeed. I expect he'll have to 'list.'

The M.C. went smiling and mincing along the parade, waving his cane jauntily, and passing his snuff-box into the other hand now and then to raise his hat to some one or another, till he turned up a side street, when, in the solitude of the empty way, he uttered a low groan, and his face changed.

'My God!' he muttered. 'How long is this miserable degradation to last?'

He looked round sharply, as if in dread lest the emotion into which he had been betrayed should have been observed, but there was no one near.

'I must try Barclay. I dare not go to Frank Burnett, for poor May's sake.'

A few minutes later he minced and rolled up to a large, heavy-looking mansion in a back street, where, beneath a great dingy portico, a grotesque satyr's head held a heavy knocker, and grinned at the visitor who made it sound upon the door.

'Hallo, Denville, you here?' said Mr. Barclay, coming up from the street. 'Didn't expect to see you. I've got the key: come in.'

' A little bit of business, my dear sir. I thought I'd come on instead of writing. Thanks—you'll pardon me—a pinch of snuff—the Prince's own mixture.'

' Ah yes.' *Snuff, snuff, snuff.* ' Don't like it though—too scented for me. Come along.'

He led the way through a large, gloomy hall, well hung with large pictures and ornamented with pedestals and busts, up a broad, well-carpeted staircase and into the drawing-room of the house—a room, however, that looked more like a museum, so crowded was it with pictures, old china, clocks, statues, and bronzes. Huge vases, tiny Dresden ornaments, rich carpets, branches and lustres of cut glass and ormolu, almost jostled each other, while the centre of the room was filled with lounges, chairs and tables, rich in buhl and marqueterie.

At a table covered with papers sat plump, pleasant-looking Mrs. Barclay, in a very rich, stiff brocade silk. Her appearance was vulgar; there were too many rings upon her fat fingers, too much jewellery about her neck and throat; and her showy cap was a wonder of lace and ribbons; but Nature had set its stamp upon her countenance, and though she was holding her head on one side, pursing up her lips and frowning as she wrote in the big ledger-like book open before her, there was no mistaking the fact that she was a thoroughly good-hearted amiable soul.

' Oh, bless us, how you startled me!' she cried, throwing

herself back, for the door had opened quietly, and steps were hardly heard upon the soft carpet. 'Why, it's you, Mr. Denville, looking as if you were just going to a ball. How are you? Not well? You look amiss. And how's Miss Claire? and pretty little Mrs. Mayblossom—Mrs. Burnett?'

'My daughters are well in the extreme, Mrs. Barclay,' said the M.C., taking the lady's plump extended hand as she rose, to bend over it, and kiss the fingers with the most courtly grace. 'And you, my dear madam, you?'

'Oh, she's well enough, Denville,' said Barclay, chuckling. 'Robust's the word for her.'

'For shame, Jo—si—ah!' exclaimed the lady, reddening furiously. She had only blushed slightly before with plea- sure; and after kicking back her stiff silk dress to make a profound curtsey. 'You shouldn't say such things. Why, Mr. Denville, I haven't seen you for ever so long; and I've meant to call on Miss Claire, for we always get on so well together; but I'm so busy, what with the servants, *and* the dusting, *and* the keeping the books, *and* the exercise as I'm obliged to take——'

'And don't,' said Barclay, placing a chair for the M.C., and then sitting down and putting his hands in his pockets.

'For shame, Jo—si—ah. I do indeed, Mr. Denville, and it do make me so hot.'

'There, that'll do, old lady. Mr. Denville wants to see me on business. Don't you, Denville?'

'Yes—on a trifle of business; but I know that Mrs. Barclay is in your confidence. You'll pardon me, Mrs. Barclay?'

A looker-on would have imagined that he was about to dance a minuet with the lady, but he delicately took her fingers by the very tip and led her back to her seat, into which she meant to glide gracefully, but plumped down in a very feather-beddy way, and then blushed and frowned.

'Oh, Mr. Denville won't mind me; and him an old neighbour, too, as knows how I keep your books and everything. It isn't as if he was one of your wicked bucks, and bloods, and macaronies as they calls 'em.'

'Now, when you've done talking, woman, perhaps you'll let Denville speak.'

'Jo—si—ah!' exclaimed the lady, reddening, or to speak more correctly, growing more red, as she raised a large fan, which hung by a silken cord, and used it furiously.

'Now then, Denville, what is it?' said Barclay, throwing himself back in his chair, and looking the extreme of vulgarity beside the visitor's refinement.

'You'll pardon me, Mr. Barclay?' said the M.C., bowing. 'Thanks. The fact is, my dear Barclay, the time has arrived when I must launch my son Morton upon the stream of the fashionable world.'

'Mean to marry him well?' said Barclay, smiling.

'Exactly. Yes. You'll pardon me.'

He took snuff in a slow, deliberate, and studied mode that Mrs. Barclay watched attentively, declaring afterwards that it was as good as a play, while her husband also took his pinch from his own box, but in a loud, rough, frill-browning way.

'I have high hopes and admirable prospects opening out before him, my dear Barclay. Fortune seems to have marked him for her own, and to have begun to smile.'

'Fickle jade, sir; fickle jade.'

'At times—you'll pardon me. At times. Let us enjoy her smiles while we can. And now, my dear Barclay, that I wish to launch him handsomely and well—to add to his natural advantages the little touches of dress, a cane and snuff-box, and such trifles—I find, through the absence of so many fashionable visitors affecting my fees, I am troubled, inconvenienced for the want of a few guineas, and—er—it is very ridiculous—er—really I did not know whom to ask, till it occurred to me that you, my dear sir, would oblige me with, say, forty or fifty upon my note of hand.'

'Couldn't do it, sir. Haven't the money. Couldn't.'

'Don't talk such stuff, Jo-si-ah,' exclaimed Mrs. Barclay, fanning herself sharply, and making a sausage-like curl wabble to and fro, and her ribbons flutter. 'You can if you like.'

'Woman!' he exclaimed furiously.

'Oh, I don't mind you saying "woman,"' retorted the

lady. 'Telling such wicked fibs, and to an old neighbour too. If it had been that nasty, sneering, snickle dandy, Sir Harry Payne, or that big, pompous, dressed-up Sir Matthew Bray, you'd have lent them money directly. I'm ashamed of you.'

'Will you allow me to carry on my business in my own way, madam ?'

'Yes, when it's with nobodies ; but I won't sit by and hear you tell our old neighbour, who wants a bit of help, that you couldn't do it, and that you haven't the money, when anybody can see it sticking out in lumps in both of your breeches' pockets, if they like to look.'

''Pon my soul, woman,' said Barclay, banging his fist down upon the table, 'you're enough to drive a man mad. Denville, that woman will ruin me.'

Mrs. Barclay shut up her fan and sat back in her chair, and there was a curious kind of palpitating throbbing perceptible all over her that was almost startling at first till her face broke up in dimples, and the red lips parted, showing her white teeth, while her eyes half-closed. For Mrs. Barclay was laughing heartily.

'Ruin him, Mr. Denville, ruin him !' she cried. 'Ha, ha, ha, and me knowing that——'

'Woman, will you hold your tongue ?' thundered Barclay. 'There, don't take any notice of what I said, Denville. I've been put out this morning and money's scarce.

You owe me sixty now and interest, besides two years' rent.'

' I do—I do, my dear sir; but really, my dear Barclay, I intend to repay you every guinea.'

' He's going to lend it to you, Mr. Denville,' said Mrs. Barclay. ' It's only his way. He always tells people he hasn't any money, and that he has to get it from his friend in the City.'

' Be quiet, woman,' said Barclay, smiling grimly. ' There, I'll let you have it, Denville. Make a memorandum of it, my gal. Let's see: how much do you want? Twenty-five will do, I suppose ?'

' My dear friend—you'll pardon me—if you could make it fifty you would confer a lasting obligation upon me. I have great hopes, indeed.'

' Fifty ? It's a great deal of money, Denville.'

' Lend him the fifty, Josiah, and don't make so much fuss about it,' said the lady, opening the ledger, after drawing her chair to the table, taking a dip of ink, and writing rapidly in a round, clear hand. ' Got a stamp?'

' Yes,' said Barclay, taking a large well-worn pocket-book from his breast, and separating one from quite a quire. ' Fill it up. Two months after date, Denville ?'

' You'll pardon me.'

' What's the use of doing a neighbour a good turn,' said Mrs. Barclay, filling up the slip of blue paper in the most business-like manner, 'and spoiling it by being so tight. " Six months —after — date — interest — at — five — per — centum "—there.'

Mrs. Barclay put her quill pen across her mouth, and, turning the bill stamp over, gave it a couple of vigorous rubs on the blotting-paper before handing it to her husband, who ran his eye over it quickly.

' Why, you've put five per cent. *per annum*,' he cried. ' Here, fill up another. Five per cent.'

' Stuff!' said Mrs. Barclay stoutly; ' are you going to charge the poor man sixty per cent.? I shan't fill up another. Here, you sign this, Mr. Denville. Give the poor man his money, Josiah.'

' Well,' exclaimed Barclay, taking a cash-box from a drawer and opening it with a good deal of noise, ' if ever man was cursed with a tyrant for a wife——'

' It isn't you. There!' cried Mrs. Barclay, taking the bill which the visitor had duly signed, and placing it in a case along with some of its kin.

' There you are, Denville,' said Barclay, counting out the money in notes, ' and if you go and tell people what a fool I am, I shall have to leave the town.'

' Not while I live, Mr. Barclay,' said the M.C., taking the notes carefully, but with an air of indolent carelessness and grace, as if they were of no account to such a man as he. ' Sir, I thank you from my very heart. You have done me a most kindly action. Mrs. Barclay, I thank you. My daughter shall thank you for this. You'll pardon me. My visit is rather short. But business. Mr. Barclay, good-day. I shall not forget this. Mrs. Barclay, your humble servant.'

He took the hand she held out by the tips of the fingers, and bent over it to kiss them with the most delicate of touches ; but somehow, just then there seemed to be a catch in his breath, and he pressed his lips firmly on the soft, fat hand.

' God bless you !' he said huskily, and he turned and left the room.

' Poor man !' said Mrs. Barclay after a few moments' pause, as she and her lord listened to the descending steps, and heard the front door close. ' Why, look here, Josiah, at my hand, if it ain't a tear.'

' Tchah ! an old impostor and sham. Wipe it off, woman, wipe it off. Kissing your hand, too, like that, before my very face.'

' No, Jo—si—ah, I don't believe he's a bad one under all his sham and fuss. Folks don't know folkses' insides. They say you are about the hard-heartedest old money-lender that ever breathed, but they don't know you as I do There, it was very good of you to let him have it, poor old man. I knew you would.'

' I've thrown fifty pounds slap into the gutter.'

' No, you haven't, dear ; you've lent it to that poor old fellow, and you've just pleased me a deal better than if you'd given me a diamond ring, and that's for it, and more to come.'

As she spoke she threw one plump arm round the money-lender's neck, and there was a sound in the room as of a smack.

CHAPTER XXV.

A REVELATION.

'Oh, May, May! As if I had not care and pain enough without this. Surely it cannot be true.'

'Hush! don't make a fuss like that, you silly thing. You'll have the people hearing you down in the street. How could I help it?'

'Help it? May, you must have been mad.'

'Oh! no, I wasn't,' said Mrs. Burnett, nestling into a corner of the couch in her father's drawing-room. 'I believe he was, though, poor fellow,'

She gazed up at her portrait with her pretty girlish face wrinkling up, and these wrinkles seeming to have had work to get the better of the dimples in her baby cheeks and chin.

'He was dreadfully fond of me, Claire,' she continued, 'and I was very fond of him. And then, you see, we were both so young.'

Claire clasped her hands together and gazed at her sister with a face full of wonder, she seemed so calm and uncon-

cerned, as if it were some one else's trouble and not her own
that had brought the tears into her eyes.

'But, May, why did not you confide in me?'

'Likely! You were always scolding and snubbing me,
as it was. I don't know what you would have said if you
had known. Besides, I was afraid of you in those days.'

'May, you will drive me mad,' said Claire, pacing the room.

'Nonsense; and don't go on running up and down the
room like that. Be sensible, and help me.'

'Why have you not told me before?'

'I've been going to tell you heaps of times, but you've
always had something or other to worry about, and I've been
put off.'

'Till you knew that detection was inevitable; and now
you come to me,' cried Claire reproachfully.

'Look here, Claire, are you going to talk sensibly, or am
I to go to some lady friend to help me? There's Mrs. Pontardent.'

'No, no,' cried Claire excitedly. 'You must not take
anyone else into your confidence. Tell me all. But May,
May, is this really true, or is it some miserable invention of
your own?'

'Oh, it's true enough,' said May sharply, as she arranged
her bonnet strings, and bent forward to catch a glimpse of
her great ostrich feather.

Claire looked at her with her face drawn with care and

horror, while she wondered at the indifference of the little wife, and the easy way in which she was trying to shift the trouble and responsibility of her weakness and folly upon her sister.

' Why, May, you could not have been seventeen.'

' Sixteen and a half,' said May. ' Heigho ! I begin to feel quite an old woman now.'

' But, Frank ? Do you ever think of the consequences if he were to know ?'

' Why, of course I do, you silly thing. Haven't I lain in bed and quaked hundreds of times for fear he should ever find out ? How can you talk so ? Why do you suppose I came to you, if it was not that I was afraid of his getting to know ?'

' May, it would drive our father mad if all came out.'

' Of course it would. Now you are beginning to wake up and understand why I have come.'

' How could you accept Frank Burnett, and deceive him so ?'

' How could I marry him ? What would papa have said if I had refused ? Don't talk stuff.'

Claire's brow knit more and more, as she realized her sister's utter want of principle, and her heart seemed rent by anger, pity, and grief.

' Besides, do you suppose I wanted to stop here and pinch and starve when a rich husband and home were waiting for me? Poor Louis was dead, and if I'd cried my eyes out every week and said I'd be a widow for ever and ever, it would not have brought him to life.'

Claire did not speak. Her words would not come, and she gazed in utter perplexity, struggling to realize the fact that the girlish little thing before her could possibly have been a widow and mother before she became Mrs. Burnett.

'When—when did this begin?' said Claire at last.

'Now, don't talk to me like that, Claire, or you'll set me off crying my eyes blind, and I shall go home red and miserable, and Frank will find it all out.'

'He must be told.'

'Told?' cried May, starting up. 'Told? If he is told, I'll go right down to the end of the pier and drown myself. He must never know, and papa must never know. Do you think I've kept this a secret for more than two years for them to be told?'

'They will be sure to know.'

'Yes, if you tell them. Oh, Claire, Claire, I did think I could find help in my sister, now that I am in such terrible trouble.'

'I will help you all I can, May,' said Claire sadly; 'but they must know.'

'I tell you they must not,' cried May angrily, and speaking like a spoiled child. 'Frank would kill me, and as for poor, dear, darling papa, with all his troubles about getting you married and Morton settled, and Fred turning out so badly, it would kill him, and then you'd have a nice time of it, far worse than poor old mummy Teigne being killed.'

'Oh, hush, May!' said Claire, with a horrified look.

'That moves you, does it, miss? Well, then, be reasonable. I don't know what to make of you of late, Claire; you seem to be so changed. Ah, you'll find the difference when you're a married woman.'

Claire gazed down at her, with the trouble and perplexity seeming to increase, while May Burnett arranged the folds of her dress, as she once more nestled in the corner of the old sofa, and seemed as if she were posing herself to be pitied and helped.

Then she lifted her eyes towards the florid portrait on the wall, and sighed.

'Poor Louis! How he did flatter me. But he always did that, and I suppose it was his flattering words made me love him so. I was very fond of him.'

'May,' said Claire excitedly, 'when was it you were married?'

'Oh, it was such fun. It was while I was staying at Aunt Jerdein's, and taking the music lessons. I went out as usual, to go to Golden Square for my lesson as aunt thought, and Louis was waiting for me, and he took me in a hackney coach with straw at the bottom and mouldy old cushions, and one of the windows broken. And we went to such a queer old church somewhere in the city, and were married—a little old church that smelt as mouldy as the hackney coach; and the funny old clergyman took snuff all over his surplice, and he did mumble so.'

' And then ?'

' Oh, Louis left Saltinville, you know, when I went up to London, and gave lessons at Aunt Jerdein's, and we used to see as much of each other as we could, till he had to go back to Rome, and there, poor boy, you know he died of fever.'

Claire did not speak, but stood with her hands clasped before her, listening to the calm, cool, selfish words that seemed to come rippling out from the prettily-curved mouth as if it were one of the simplest and most matter-of-fact things in the world.

' It was a great trouble to me, of course, dear,' May continued ; and she raised herself a little, to spread her handsome dress, so that it should fall in graceful folds. ' I used to cry my eyes out, and I don't know what I should have done if it had not been for Anne Brown.'

' Anne Brown? Aunt Jerdein's servant ?' said Claire bitterly. ' You trusted her, then, in preference to your own sister.'

' No, I didn't, baby. She found me out. And besides, I daren't have told you. How you would have scolded me, you know,' continued May. ' Anne was very good to me,

and I went and stayed with her mother when baby was
born, and then Anne left aunt soon after. Aunt thought,
you know, that I'd come down home, and, of course, you
all thought I was still at aunt's. Anne Brown managed
about the letters.'

' Go on,' said Claire, who listened as if this were all some
horrible fiction that she was forced to hear.

' Then I did come home, and Anne Brown took care of
poor baby with her mother, and it was terribly hard work to
get money to send them, but somehow I did it; and then
you know about Frank Burnett, how poor dear papa brought
all that on.'

Claire uttered a sigh that was almost a groan, but the
pretty little rosebud of a wife went prattling on, in selfish
ignorance of the agony she was inflicting, dividing her attention between her dress and the picture of herself that was
smiling down at her from the wall.

' I suffered very much all that time, Claire dear, and,
whenever I could, I used to go upstairs, lock myself in my
room, and put on a little widow's cap I had—a very small
one, dear, of white crape—and have a good cry about poor
Louis. It was the only mourning I ever could wear for him,
and it was nearly always locked up in the bottom drawer ;
but I used to carry a bit of black crape in my dress pocket,
and touch that now and then. It was a little strip put
through my wedding ring and tied in a knot. There it is,'

she said, fishing it out of her dress pocket; ' but the strip of crape only looks like a bit of black rag now.'

She held out a tiny, plain gold ring for her sister to see, and it looked so small that it seemed as if it had been used sometime when a little girl had been playing at being married with some little boy, or at one of the child weddings that history records.

' Poor Louis !' sighed May. ' I was very fond of him. Then, when I was married again, of course I was able to send money up every week easily enough till Frank began to grow so stingy, when I've often had no end of trouble to get it together. But I always have managed somehow. Oh, dear me ! This is a wearisome place, this world.'

Claire stood gazing down at her, and May went on :

' Then all went smoothly enough till that stupid Anne's mother took a cold or something, and died; then Anne sent me word that she was going to be married, and I must fetch poor baby away.'

The sisters' eyes now met as May continued :

' So, as I didn't know anyone else, I went to Mrs. Miggles out there on the cliff, and told her how I was situated. She wouldn't help me at first. She said I was to tell you; but when I told her I dared not, and promised her I'd pay her very regularly, she came round, and she went up to London by the coach and fetched baby, and a great expense it was to me, for she had to come back inside. Do open the window, Claire ; this room is stifling.'

Claire slowly crossed the room and threw open the window and then returned to stand gazing at her sister.

' And your little innocent child is there at that fisherman's hut on the cliff ?'

' Yes, dear,' said May calmly ; and then, for the first time, her face lit up, and she showed some trace of feeling as she exclaimed :

' And, oh, Claire dear, she is such a little darling.'

Claire looked at her in a strangely impassive way. It was as if the story she had heard of her sister's weakness and deception had stunned her, and, instead of looking at her, she gazed right away with wistful eyes at the past troubles culminating in Fred's enlistment, and then that horror, the very thought of which sent a shudder through her frame.

And now this new trouble had come, one that might prove a terrible disgrace, while the future looked so black that she dared not turn her mental gaze in that direction.

' Well,' said May, at last, ' why don't you speak—though you need not, if you are only going to scold.'

' Why have you come to tell me this now—this disgraceful story of deceit and shame ?'

' Do you wish to send me back broken-hearted, Claire— crying my eyes out so that Frank is sure to know ?'

' I say, why have you come to me, May ?'

'Because I am in dreadful trouble at last, and don't know what to do. I daren't communicate with those people or go near the cottage, for I'm sure Frank is watching me and suspecting something.'

'You will have to confess everything, May; he loves you and will forgive you.'

'But he doesn't love me, and he never would forgive me,' cried May excitedly. 'You can't think how we quarrel. He's a horribly jealous little monster, and I hate him.'

'May!'

'I don't care: I do. Now, look here, Claire, it's of no use for you to boggle about it, because you must help me. If it were to come out it would be social ruin for us all, and I've had quite enough poverty, thank you. I dare not go and see the little thing again, and if some one does not take the Miggleses some money regularly, likely as not they'll turn disagreeable and begin to talk. I shall bring you money, of course, and as some one must go and see that my poor darling is properly cared for, why you must.'

'I?'

'Yes, dear, you. The poor little thing shall not be neglected, I'm determined upon that; and as my situation prevents me, why it is your duty, Claire.'

'Who knows that this is your little girl, May?' said Claire coldly.

'Nobody.'

'Not even the fisherman's wife?'

'Well, I dare say she thinks something; but those people never say anything so long as you pay them regularly. But there, I dare not stay any longer. There's a guinea, Claire; it's all I have to-day. Take that to Mrs. Miggles, and see how the darling is. I must be off. I'll come in to-morrow and hear.'

'May, I cannot—I dare not—try to cloak this shameful story.'

'But you must, I tell you. Now, don't be so silly. Why, I'd do as much for you.'

'I tell you I dare not do this. I must tell papa—or, there, I'll be your help in this; I'll come with you, and you shall confess to Frank.'

'Why, he'd kill me. I know it has been a surprise to you, and you are a bit taken aback, but think about it, and you will see that it is your duty to help me now. Good-bye, Claire dear,' she continued, as she kissed her sister. 'Nobody knows anything about this but you, and it is our secret, mind. Good-bye.'

Claire hardly heard the door close as May rustled out of the room, hot and excited by the confidence she had had to make, but evidently quite at her ease, as her bright eyes and smile showed, when she looked up from her carriage and nodded at her sister.

Claire looked down at her, drawn involuntarily to the

window; and as the carriage drove off, and she still remained gazing straight before her, an officer passed and raised his hat.

Claire had an instinctive feeling that it was Major Rockley, but she neither looked nor moved, for the face of a tiny child seemed to be looking up at her, smiling, and asking her sympathy.

Then she started into life as there was another footstep on the boulder path, and another hat was raised, and an eager appealing look met hers, making her shrink hastily away, with her erst blank face growing agitated as she drew back trembling and fighting hard to keep down the sobs that rose.

For all that was past now for her. With the secrets she had held within her breast before, how dared she to think of his love? Now there was another—a secret so fraught with future trouble that she hardly dared dwell upon all that she had heard. It had come upon her that morning like a thunderclap—this new trouble, known only to herself and the fisherman's wife. So May had said: for she had gone to her sister to demand her aid in happy ignorance of this part of her miserable story being known, beside much more, to little library-keeping Miss Clode.

CHAPTER XXVI.

'Who is it?'

'It's that Major Rockley, Jo-si-ah, and he's walking up and down, switching his riding-whip about, and he'll be knocking down some of the chiney if you don't make haste.'

'Let him wait a minute,' said Barclay, finishing a letter.

'I do 'ate that man, Jo-si-ah—that I do,' said Mrs. Barclay.

'I wish you wouldn't talk so, old lady, when I'm writing.'

'I can't help it, Jo-si-ah. That man, whenever I meet him, makes me begin to boil. So smooth, and polite, and smiling, and squeeze-your-handy, while all the while he's laughing at you for being so fat.'

'Laughing at me for being so fat?'

'No, no. You know what I mean—laughing at me myself for being so fat. I 'ate him.'

'Well, I don't want you to love him, old lady.'

'I should think not, indeed, with his nasty dark eyes and his long black mustarchers. Ugh! the monster. I 'ate him.'

'Handsomest man in Saltinville, my dear.'

'Handsome is as handsome does, Jo-si-ah. He's a black-hearted one, if ever there was one, I know.'

'Now, you don't know anything of the kind, old girl.'

'Oh, yes, I do, Jo-si-ah. I always feel it whenever he comes anigh one, and if I had a child of my own, and that man had come and wanted to marry her, I'd have cut her up in little pieces and scattered them all about the garden first.'

'Well, then, I suppose I ought to be very, very glad that we never had any little ones, for, though I should be very glad to get rid of you——'

'No, you wouldn't, Jo-si-ah,' said Mrs. Barclay, showing her white teeth.

'Yes, I should, but I shouldn't have liked to see you hung for murder.'

'Don't talk like that, Jo-si-ah. It gives me the shivers. That word makes me think about old Lady Teigne, and not being safe in my bed.'

'Stuff and nonsense!'

'It isn't stuff and nonsense, Jo-si-ah. I declare, ever since that dreadful affair, I never see a bolster without turning cold all down my back; and I feel as if it wasn't safe to put my head upon my pillow of a night. There: he's ringing because you're so long.'

'Then I shall be longer,' growled Barclay, putting a wafer in his mouth.

'How that poor Claire Denville can stop in that house of a night I don't know.'

'Ah, that puts me in mind of something: I wish you wouldn't be so fond of that Claire Denville.'

'Why not? I must be fond of somebody.'

'Be fond of me, then, I'm ugly enough.'

'So I am fond of you, Jo-si-ah, and you are not ugly, and I should like to hear anyone say you were to my face.'

'I don't like that Denville lot.'

'No more do I, Jo-si-ah, only poor dear Claire. Her father ain't bad, but she's as good as gold.'

'I don't know so much about that,' muttered Barclay.

'And now, Jo-si-ah, just you be careful with that Major Rockley. He owes you a lot now.'

'Yes, but I've got him tight enough.'

'And if you let him have more you get him tighter. He's a bold, bad man, always gambling and drinking, and doing worse.'

'Oh, I'm very fond of him, old lady,' said Barclay, chuckling. 'I love him like a son, and—there he is again. I must go now.'

It was only into the next room, but there were double doors, and as Barclay entered the Major's countenance did not look at all handsome, but very black and forbidding.

'Come, Barclay,' he cried, with a smile; 'I thought you were going to put me off. Here, I've been hard hit again. I'm as poor as Job, and I must have a hundred.'

For answer Barclay shrugged his shoulders, took out a fat pocket-book, and began to draw out the tuck.

'Put that away,' cried the Major impatiently; and he gave the book a flick with his riding-whip, but not without cutting right across Barclay's fingers, and making a red mark.

The money-lender did not even wince, but he mentally made a mark against his client's name, intimating that the cut would have to be paid for some day or another.

'I know all about that. I've had five hundred of you during the past two months. Never mind that; the luck must turn sometime. Cards have been dead against me lately. That Mellersh has the most extraordinary luck; but I shall have him yet, and we'll soon be square again. Come, I want a hundred.'

'When?'

'Now, man, now.'

'Can't be done, Major, really.'

'Don't talk nonsense, man. I tell you I must have it.'

'Your paper's getting bad, Major. Too much of it in the market.'

'Look here, Barclay; do you want to insult me?'

'Not I, sir; never thought of such a thing.'

'Then what do you mean?'

'I mean? Only that you've had five hundred pounds of my money during these last three months.'

'For which you hold bills for seven hundred and fifty.'

'You put down five hundred pounds now in Bank of England notes, Major Rockley, and you shall have the lot.'

'Then you do mean to insult me, sir?'

'No, Major.'

'What do you mean, then?'

'Only that I won't part with another five-pound note till I get some of that money back.'

Major Rockley's dark brows came down over his eyes as he glared at Barclay with a peculiarly vindictive expression, while the money-lender thrust his hands deep down into his drab breeches' pockets, and whistled softly.

'I shall not forget this, Barclay,' he said slowly, and, turning upon his heels, he walked out of the place beating his boot viciously with his whip.

'Oh, the monster!' cried Mrs. Barclay, entering the room.

'Why, you've been listening.'

'Well, didn't you leave the door open on purpose for me to listen, Jo-si-ah? Oh, what a bad, evil-looking man, Jo-si-ah. I believe he wouldn't stop at anything to get money from you now.'

'Black mask and a pair of pistols, on a dark night in a

country road, eh, old lady? Stand and deliver; money or
your life, eh?'

'Well, you may laugh, Jo-si-ah; but he looks just the
sort of man who wouldn't stop at anything. I am glad you
wouldn't let him have any money, for I'm sure you'd never
get it back.'

'I don't know so much about that, old lady, but whether
or no, I wasn't going to let him have any this morning. He
has been short lately, and no mistake. Some one I know's
making a nice thing out of them at the mess.'

'Colonel Mellersh?'

'Mum!'

'Oh, there's no one to hear us now. But, I say, Jo-si-ah,
why is he so friendly with Miss Clode?'

'Because she sells packs of cards, old girl.'

'Ah, but there's something more than that. I went in
there one day, and he had hold of her hand across the
counter; and I could see, though she turned it off, that she
had been crying.'

'Asking her to wed, and let him succeed to the business,'
said Barclay, with a chuckle.

'Don't talk nonsense, Jo-si-ah. I wish I had a good,
clear head like you, and was as clever, and then perhaps I
could make this out.'

'What?'

'About Miss Clode. I'm sure she has seen better days.'

'That she has,' said Barclay, chuckling.   'She looks
pretty shabby now, a newsy, gossiping old hag!'

'I don't dislike Miss Clode,' said Mrs. Barclay thoughtfully.   'There's much worse in Saltinville.'

'I dare say,' he said, laughing.

'I've only one thing against her.'

'What's that?'

'She hates poor Claire Denville like poison.'

CHAPTER XXVII.

FISHERMAN DICK STARES.

Major Rockley had counted upon getting a hundred pounds from Barclay, and the refusal annoyed him to so great an extent that he determined upon having a sharp walk to calm himself. So setting off at a good rate towards the main cliff to reach the downs beyond the town, he had not gone far before he saw a graceful figure, in a white dress, with black scarf and plain straw bonnet going in the same direction.

'Claire Denville as I'm a sinner!' he cried, his pale cheeks flushing, and a curious light shining in his dark eyes.

'Yes, without doubt,' he muttered. 'Off for a walk to the downs. Lucky accident. At last!'

He checked himself, walking slowly, so as not to overtake her until she was well out of the town, and thinking that perhaps it would be as well to keep back until she turned, and then meet her face to face.

'The jade! How she has kept me at a distance. Re-

fused my notes, and coquetted with me to make me more
eager for the pursuit. The old man's lessons have not been
thrown away. I'm to approach in due form, I suppose.
Well, we shall see.'

Claire went straight on, walking pretty quickly, and
without turning her head to right or left. The streets
were left behind; the row of houses facing the sea
had come to an end; and she was getting amongst the
fishermen's cottages, while below the cliff the fishing boats
were drawn high up on the shingle, and long, brown filmy
ets spread out to dry, looking like square shadows cast by
invisible sails, and mingled with piles of tarred barrels,
lobster baskets, and brown ropes, bladders and corks.

Every here and there, on the railing at the cliff edge,
hung oilskins to soften in the sunshine, and in one place a
giant appeared to be sitting astride the rail, with nothing to be
seen of him but a huge pair of boots. Farther on fish were
drying in the air, and farther still there came up a filmy
cloud of grey smoke from the shingle, along with a pleasant
smell of Stockholm tar, for Fisherman Dick was busy paying
the bottom of a boat turned upside down below the cliff.

These matters did not interest Major Rockley any more
than the grey gulls that wheeled overhead and descended,
to drop with a querulous cry upon a low spit of shingle
where the sea was retiring fast.

For the fluttering white dress took up all his attention,

and now that they were well beyond the promenaders, he was about to hasten his steps—too impatient to wait until she turned—when he uttered an impatient oath, for Claire suddenly stopped by a cottage where a woman was sitting knitting a coarse blue garment and nursing a little child.

It was all so sudden that it took the officer by surprise. The woman jumped up hastily on being spoken to, and curtseyed, and they went in at once, leaving the Major by the rails.

'Well, I can wait,' he said, smiling and taking out his cigar-case. 'I can study the tarring of boats till her lady-ship appears.'

He slowly chose and lit a cigar, and then, going close to the edge of the cliff, leaned upon the rails and gazed down at Fisherman Dick, who was working away busily, dipping his brush in a little three-legged iron pot, and carefully spreading the dark-brown odorous tar.

He was about forty feet below the Major, and for some time he went on steadily with his work, but all at once he stopped short, and turned his face upwards as if he felt that he was being watched; and as he did so his straw hat fell off and he stood fixed by the Major's eyes as if unable to move.

The sensation was mutual, for Major Rockley felt attracted by the dark, Spanish-looking face, and the keen eyes so intently fixed upon his.

'Confound the fellow! how he stares,' said the Major, at

last, as he seemed to wrench himself away, and turned his back.

As he did so, leaning against the rail, Dick Miggles drew a long breath, stared now at his iron tar-kettle, and carried it to the fire of old wreck-wood to re-heat it, as he stood by and thoughtfully scratched his head.

He looked up for a moment, and saw that the Major's back was towards him, and then bent over his kettle again, and began pushing half-burned scraps of wood beneath, making the fire roar and the pitch heat quickly, and he did not look up again till the Major had walked away, when he began to brush again at the boat as if relieved, ending by giving one leg a tremendous slap, and stopping short as if to think.

The Major had some time to wait, and he passed a good deal of it walking up and down, as if watching a sail in the offing, till fortune favoured him; so that as he was approaching the cottage again, Claire came out quickly, and, seeing him, started and turned to walk in the other direction, out on the downs and round by the London Road into the town.

She repented on the instant, and wished that she had faced him boldly and passed on. But she was excited and confused by her visit, which had to her a curious suggestion of wrong-doing in it; and she was leaving the place, feeling agitated and guilty, when, seeing the Major, she had turned sharply to walk on, trembling, and hoping that he had not seen her. The hope died out on the instant, for she heard his steps, with the soft *clink*, *clink* of the rowels of his spurs ; but he kept his distance till they were well beyond the cottages, and then rapidly closed up.

What would he think of her visit there ? What would he say? were the questions Claire asked herself as she walked rapidly on to reach the stile that bounded the cornfield she would have to turn into and cross to get into the London Road ; and all the time, *clink*, *clink*—*clink*, *clink*, those spurs rang on her ears, and came nearer and nearer.

The stile at last ; and, trembling with eagerness, she was about to cross, when the Major passed her quickly, leaped over, and turned smilingly to face her with :

' Allow me, my dear Miss Denville. We meet at last.'

END OF VOL. I.

BILLING AND SONS, PRINTRS, GUILDFORD.